Celestial Seasonings

Also by Helen Muir

DON'T CALL IT LOVE
NOUGHTS AND CROSSES
THE BELLES LETTRES OF ALEXANDRA BONAPARTE
MANY MEN AND TALKING WIVES
NOTHING FOR YOU, LOVE
CONSEQUENCES

Celestial Seasonings

HELEN MUIR

SIMON & SCHUSTER
LONDON · SYDNEY · NEW YORK · TOKYO · SINGAPORE · TORONTO

First published in Great Britain by Simon & Schuster Ltd, 1995
A Paramount Communications Company

Copyright © Helen Muir, 1995

This book is copyright under the Berne Convention.
No reproduction without permission.
All rights reserved.

The right of Helen Muir to be identified as author of this work has been asserted in accordance with sections 77 and 78 of the Copyright, Designs and Patents Act 1988.

Simon & Schuster Ltd
West Garden Place
Kendal Street
London W2 2AQ

Simon & Schuster of Australia Pty Ltd
Sydney

A CIP catalogue record for this book is available from the British Library

ISBN 0-671-71850-9

'My Dearest Dear' by Ivor Novello
© Chappell Music Ltd, 1939
reproduced by kind permission of International Music Publications Ltd

Typeset in Goudy Modern 14/15pt by
Palimpsest Book Production Limited, Polmont, Stirlingshire
Printed and bound in Great Britain by
Butler & Tanner Ltd, Frome & London

With love to Margaret, Laszlo and Lindy

A good name is better than precious ointment: and the day of death than the day of one's birth.

                              Ecclesiastes VII. v.i.

ONE

'Never *never* let a man touch your bust!' It was ten past four in the morning in 1953 when Mrs Welsh coined this historic new warning maxim for her teenage daughter, Rosemary, who had just got home from a dance which she knew had ended at one o'clock.

As usual, her widowed mother had lain awake waiting for her. Now, she was out of bed and prowling about the landing, looking like an embattled hen tea-cosy in her hairnet and bulky old brown wool dressing gown. The row about where Roz had been until this hour erupted immediately. The dialogue took its normal course. Mrs Welsh, her face disfigured with accusation and anxiety, let fly with a torrent of words as furious as if a catastrophe had already occurred.

'If you behave like a silly little loose ass, you'll get yourself talked about all over the district and once you've got a bad name, you're done for. You can never live it down. Never! The girls who cheapen themselves with boys are not respected by them. The boys laugh, of course, behind their backs, but there are always a few scum girls, who can't get a boy, who think its the thing to sit in cars after dances kissing and giggling and letting boys put their hands down inside their dresses . . .'

'Oh poof!' Roz said, lolling on the stairs with a defiant, tipsy smile. 'Well, I don't.'

'No, never you let a man touch your bust, dear. That's the end. You don't want to let yourself become a laughing stock.'

'People must be very easily amused.'

'Oh yes, they're amused all right, if someone makes a fool of herself, make no mistake about that. Word gets round like wildfire. *Like wildfire*! The whole district hears of it. I don't want you to get a scum name because there's nothing in the world a man admires more than a good woman.' Carried away with this hypothesis, Mrs Welsh repeated it, altering the picture slightly and suddenly assuming a most spectacular expression of saintliness, as though she was speaking from personal experience. 'And of course there is nothing a *bad* man respects more than a good woman,' she added, with even more feeling and a far-away smile. 'The bad man absolutely reveres her!'

It was as if, Roz thought, a trail of wasters had been transformed in her mother's own hands. 'I'll leave the bad men to you then,' she said, 'I don't want one.'

Mrs Welsh never flagged in these skirmishes. After the initial attack, she kept up an easy rhythm until she got the last word. 'A bad man, dear, is all you may get if you're not very careful. Once your name is blackened . . .'

'My name is not black. What on earth are you talking about?' Roz shouted after her as her mother went into the lavatory. She stepped up to the top of the stairs to be nearer to the open door. 'Nobody has ever touched my bust because I don't want them to. But if I *did* I'd let 'em. Got that?'

'Don't be rude.'

'Are you listening?'

'I'm listening, dear,' Mrs Welsh replied evenly, pulling the chain, 'I was only trying to give you a warning.'

'I don't need any warnings, thank you. Anyway, I've met a blissful man. He's a musical star and he brought me home but you've spoilt everything now.'

Her mother gave a doubtful laugh as she emerged. 'Not another band leader, I hope! I want you to find a decent boy.'

Roz stalked off to her bedroom mouthing angrily to herself. 'Oh, shut up,' she said, sotto voce. She kicked off her red satin shoes and flung her tiny sequinned bag across the room. 'He is not in a band, as a matter of fact, but what if he was? That wouldn't make him indecent, would it? He is only the leading man in the Manchester Operatic Society and a flight lieutenant. He's just coming out of the RAF. I don't know what you mean by decent. Decent? Who are these decent people you're always on about? Where are they?'

Winifred Welsh came to the door of her room and stood pondering just inside it. 'I only mean the families with a bit of breed. Yes, I must say I don't imagine there are many of the decent people left in this district.' She gave a wistful sigh. 'I don't know what's happened to them. I expect they've all probably inter-married with the yoiks by now and there aren't any left.'

Roz laughed. 'Inter-married with the yoiks!' she repeated, delighted, and then her mother laughed with her. She suddenly looked white-faced and exhausted because it was already beginning to get light. Roz felt contrite and kissed her.

'His name is Ivor Mostance.'

Her mother nodded. 'I'm sure I know Mrs Mostance by

sight. A bit of a stamper She's theatrical-looking, mutton dressed lamb really with dyed hair and quite pleased with herself. Lower middle, you know. I think she belongs to the music group at the Townswomen. Is Ivor nice?'

'Ma, he is divine! He danced with me seven times. When he did the charleston, I nearly died with joy. He's the absolute champion at it. He says he's going to Anne Harvey's dance on Saturday.'

'In that case, you'd better get to bed or you'll have terrible bags under your eyes. I think you ought to wear your strapless blue for the Harvey's, but it needs a good press. I'll do it tomorrow for you. I hope there aren't any evil marks on it? You'll look your very best in that for dancing with Ivor!' And Mrs Welsh hitched up her dressing gown and charlestoned along the landing to her bedroom, giving her daughter a conspiratorial little smile over her shoulder.

TWO

The carpet in the Harveys' long drawing room had been removed and Jan Barker's five-piece band was tucked neatly into the bay window. Nearly everybody had Jan Barker at their dances, for coming out and then the twenty-first birthdays. Sometimes, round about Christmas time, Roz would see her at different houses or hotels two or three times in one week and always wearing the same red frilly blouse and long black skirt. Now, buxom jovial Jan sat up straight-backed and smiling at the piano as she thumped it out.

> *You're the cream in my coffee*
> *You're the salt in my stew . . .*

She gave her usual pleasant little nod of greeting and Roz beamed back, gratified to be recognised as a well-known party-goer. She had joined a group of girls she knew but she was praying for someone to ask her to dance before Ivor Mostance walked in. Her palms were sticky although she was feeling cold with excitement at the thought of seeing him again.

While she tried to make coherent conversation, she could

hardly keep her eyes off the doorway and then, suddenly, he was there, filling it, looking very tall and self-assured in his dinner jacket, with a midnight-blue cummerbund. He stood back to let Caroline Paul pass in first and Roz's heart sank as it always did when she found Caroline had been invited. She was the one girl every man in the room wanted to dance with. They flocked round her all night.

The fact that she was so popular with men didn't stop the women liking her too because she was such fun. Caroline shared a flat in London now and it showed. With her white complexion, dark eyes, smooth dark hair and gold nail polish, she was in another league of smartness and sophistication. Tonight it looked as if all she'd done was to throw a gorgeously-painted silk shawl round her slender boyish body. The effect was stunning. Nobody else had such careless chic. But Caroline had always been an instigator, since childhood days when she used to arrive at tea parties in beautifully-cut grey shorts, while all her contemporaries bumbled about as usual in their smocked dresses and elasticated dancing pumps.

Now Ivor was handing Caroline a drink and Mrs Harvey was introducing them into a group of people. He was older than most of the other men in the room and he seemed much more mature. His manners were better. Roz had to stop herself gazing at him like a stuffed owl. She turned her back.

But she was still aware of Ivor's deep theatrical voice and she could hear them laughing together. When she looked round again, she caught his eye. He gave her a long teasing sleepy stare, down his long straight operatic star nose, and slowly inclined his head. She was gawping back in such a bewitched state that she actually jumped at a shrill-voiced greeting called out behind her. 'Roz! Hullo . . . how are you?'

'Oh please God! Not now.' It was Daphne Phelps-Phillips, a frump, with a pasty moon face, whose parents were friends of her mother's.

'How are you, Roz?'

'Very well, thank you,' she admitted reluctantly. 'How are you?'

'Fine!' Daphne was talking in a hearty party voice as if to convince herself she was fine. She was looking a bit pig-like in pink net with a purple mohair stole round her shoulders. The skirt of her insipid girlish dress was stuffed out with stiff petticoats like a pantomime fairy. All she needed, Roz thought, was a wand. 'Go away!' she wanted to say to her, 'Get out of my way!' Why did these clinging deadbeats always have to waylay her at the wrong moments? Now she would have to arrange tennis with Daphne, to please her mother, or ask her to have lunch with her at the Kardomah.

'How's your mother?' Daphne's hair was crimped into an old-fashioned iron style and she had the doomed air of a natural wallflower – relieved to find another.

Strike me pink! Who cares how my mother is? Roz mumbled and shifted surreptitiously so she could see what Ivor was doing. Why didn't he come and get her?

'How's your mother?' Daphne repeated with even more fervent brightness.

'She's yapping her head off.'

'Roz, d'you mean she's not well?'

'She's well all right. Very strong. How's yours?'

'Let's go and sit down, shall we?' Daphne shouted. 'Come

over here, Roz. I can't hear a word you're saying while we're standing so close to the band.'

> *S'wonderful, s'marvellous*
> *You should care for me . . .*

To her utter horror, Daphne led the way into the far corner of the room and plumped herself down so that Roz had to take a chair which put her virtually out of sight. She could scarcely speak with annoyance. Now Ivor was dancing with Caroline Paul who looked at least twenty-five to night and radiant. They were whispering together. It certainly didn't look as if he was telling her he was a womaniser which was how he'd introduced himself to her. He'd sat down beside her saying: 'Hullo, my name's Ivor Mostance. I'm a womaniser.' And his mouth had quirked up at the corner in a most seductive manner.

She'd replied: 'Well don't come near me. I'm of a very nervous disposition.' She'd relived this wondrously witty exchange a hundred times.

'Would you like to dance?'

A young fair-haired boy with a beaky face which was spotty and serious was standing in front of them. Praise the Saints, he was looking straight at her.

'Thank you,' she replied, grateful for any escape. 'Excuse me a minute, Daphne.'

As they shuffled off awkwardly into a waltz, Ivor and Caroline spun past in perfect harmony.

'Tim Benstead.'

'Roz Welsh.'

'How d'you do.'

They danced in silence until Tim asked, 'Are you still at school?'

'No, actually I've left.'

'Where did you go?'

'A ghastly place in Yorkshire called Firth House. You won't have heard of it probably.'

'No, I haven't.'

'My mother chose it because of it's awfulness. It's very small and the emphasis is on good manners, character etc. You know the sort of thing . . . *Be Good Sweet Maid And Let Who Will Be Clever.*'

'Were you good?'

'I was bored stiff. I sometimes have bad dreams about being trapped in there again.' She didn't add that she'd been expelled for driving the headmistress's Ford Popular up and down the school park. Her mother said she had to try and live that down. 'It doesn't do to tell people everything. Keep your own counsel.'

'I'm in my final year at Stowe. It's not too bad.'

'I'm glad to hear it.'

She couldn't think of anything more to say to him. If Ivor Mostance fell in love with Caroline, her life would be over.

Tim twirled her rather clumsily under his arm. 'I suppose you're doing domestic science, are you?'

'No. Why should I be? I don't like cooking.'

'That's what all you girls seem to do. Either that or a secretarial course.'

She certainly wasn't going to admit that she was already ignominiously attending Miss Straker's Secretarial College, learning to type to a record of the Darktown Strutters' Ball with a sheet of paper over her hands. 'I'm a freelance brain surgeon,' she said.

He twirled her again. 'You don't look tall enough to me to be a brain surgeon.'

'It doesn't matter what size you are. They take anybody these days.'

'In that case,' he declared, eyeing her most warmly, 'I'd like a frontal lobotomy, please.'

Roz laughed. And laughed again in case Ivor Mostance was watching.

The music stopped and they stayed together. When it started again, they went on dancing. After three more dances, she suggested they stop for a rest. The conversation with Tim amused her but his youthfulness was damaging to her image. She left him and went upstairs to find a bathroom.

She locked the door and sat down to think on the lavatory seat. Oh hell, cripes. What was she to do? She bit her thumb nail and four layers of red polish cracked and peeled off. Damn! And damn, damn, damn Caroline Paul. She looked at her watch. This evening wasn't turning out as she'd expected at all. She'd been so certain Ivor would make a bee-line for her. She'd thought they'd dance and dance together until he took her home. The fact that he'd gone off with Caroline had totally taken the wind out of her sails. How on earth could she keep on beaming at everybody when she was done in with disappointment? She felt like leaving now. She picked up a copy of *Reader's Digest* lying on the window sill with *Punch* and *The Wide World*, and read the snippets from 'Life's Like That' until somebody turned the handle of the bathroom door.

She stood up and hesitated then she said 'Go to hell' under her breath and sat down again, her legs apart and her head in her hands, while she decided what to do.

A few minutes later the door handle was rattled again.

'Coming!' she called out in a hearty voice like Daphne Phelps-Phillips and got out her lipstick. She'd just have to grit her teeth and make the best of it. What if she was sitting with Daphne all night? What she could do was present herself to Mrs Harvey with a few gracious words telling her she'd sprained her ankle. That would go down well, then she could go home. She'd have to go home if Ivor was having supper with Caroline. How, she did not know because she had no money with her. Walk, probably. She went on fiddling with her hair – pushing and patting each Lollobrigida-like strand into its exact position on her forehead. She knew she looked all right. Next to Caroline, she was the prettiest there. But what if nobody liked the look of her?

She limped down the stairs into the hall where somebody had dressed up the stag's head on the wall with a cap and scarf. As she looked about for Anne's mother, there was a tap on her shoulder.

'Miss Welsh,' Ivor Mostance murmured, his mouth quirking bewitchingly, 'where have you been? I thought you must be having a bath up there. Are we going to dance?'

Smiling radiantly, limp forgotten, she led the way to the dancing.

'You look even more beautiful tonight.'

'How kind of you.' Was Caroline the *most* beautiful?

'I thought you'd forgotten all about me.'

What! 'Of course I hadn't forgotten,' she answered smoothly.

He took her hands as they moved off to the music and

folded her against him. 'So my heart is still safe in your hands, is it?'

She was going to try and nip this lofty flirtatiousness in the bud. He wasn't being serious enough for her liking.

'I didn't know you had a heart. You told me you were a womaniser.'

A quickstep with Ivor was heaven. He was such a good dancer. She felt at one with him, alive and light. At times her feet hardly seemed to touch the ground. Dancing with him was like flying.

By the time the band broke into the charleston, they were so pleased with themselves they were ready to go right over the top. Roz knew they were showing off but she was too excited to stop. A glass of fruit cup took flight from a table top as they charlestoned past. Daphne called out 'They're playing your tune, Roz!' then she slipped and fell heavily against her partner taking him down with her. Mr and Mrs Harvey watched with subdued smiles, anxiously totting up the likely damage to their parquet floor.

Roz knew how her dress swung out to show her legs because she'd practised the steps in front of her long bedroom mirror. Gradually other people stopped dancing and stood back to watch. When the music stopped, the whole room clapped them.

Ivor kissed her hand and she curtsied to him. As he led her off to sit down, they passed Caroline Paul. She was applauding too and smiling but her eyes followed Ivor and there was puzzlement in them. Maybe, Roz thought, with a tiny thrill of triumph, the number one woman had simply assumed a right to the number one man. Behind her she seemed to hear the words '... cradle snatching' spoken in Caroline's clear voice but she was not sure whether she'd really heard that or not.

Anyway, Ivor took her home that night in his little green MG, not Caroline. After the charleston, he remained attentive. She only caught him looking at Caroline once. If she was more in love with him than ever by the end of the evening, she scarcely knew him any better. All she knew was that he was the most exciting man she'd ever met in her life.

What she enjoyed, of course, was his self-assurance. All the lordly teasing and deep worldly glances. He was so quick to act if she needed anything – to find her a chair or fill up her glass. It made her feel old and sophisticated when he lit her Cocktail Sobranies with one swift attentive flick from his lighter. He called her 'an affected little thing' for smoking coloured cigarettes and that pleased her too.

At supper time he led her to a satisfyingly quiet corner. He asked her lots of questions – she hoped he was establishing her suitability to be his love – but he gave away precious little about himself. The fact that he was enigmatic made him more of a challenge and only added to his charm. He had just brought her a second helping of ice-cream when Roz suddenly saw that Daphne was sitting by herself.

'Come over here, Daphne.'

Daphne really had hurt her ankle when she fell on the floor. To Roz's relief Ivor was pleasant to her; some men scarcely bothered to hide their lack of interest. He eyed her fairy-queen net and sturdy swollen leg in its silver sandle with amiable forbearance.

'What do you do with yourself, Daphne?'

'What do I do with myself? Well, Ivor, I try to lead a

full and interesting life, you know.' Her voice was jaunty because she was so frightened of him.

His attention was diverted by a commotion across the room where Anne Harvey was egging on some of the rugger team to pour a flask of brandy into her mother's benign fruit cup.

Roz said: 'Oh, Ivor look, let's have some of that.'

'No. You're quite outrageous enough already.'

'Come on. It'll be good for Daphne's ankle.'

'Oh, I don't want any of that, thank you,' Daphne retorted quickly.

Emboldened by Daphne sitting there like a frump, Roz said. 'Well, I do,' and in her over-excited state, she stood up to get some for herself while Ivor groaned. 'I suppose I'll have to take you home now. You'll be insensible.'

She laughed at him. 'Weren't you going to anyway? You were!'

She regaled them then with an anecdote of a carless boy who had asked her to go to the pictures. Too late she'd discovered that, horror of horrors, his mother was going to act as chauffeur. With the mother at the wheel, making polite enquiries about her mother, she and the boy rode off to the Plaza together, squirming self-consciously about on the back seat of the family Humber. They sat stiffly to attention in a double seat to see *Monsieur Hûlot's Holiday*, but after her bra strap fell right down her arm, she could no longer take the film in. His mother was waiting outside like a taxi to take them home again.

At just on seventeen, Roz couldn't be doing with any more outings like this. These hairless mites of her own age were of no interest to her except as a reassuring barometer of her appeal, whereas Ivor Mostance was a man. The point was, he was in control.

On the drive home, she leant her whirling head back against the seat, basking silently in the romantic rapture of the evening, as they whizzed along the empty roads. The racing get-a-way roar from the sports car's straight-through exhaust floated away behind them on the sharp early morning air.

Anne Harvey's dance was the best dance she'd ever been to. Filled with divine moments like that charleston; dancing cheek to cheek with Ivor in the dark while the band was playing 'Smoke Gets In Your Eyes'; Tim Benstead offering her a dish of dates and saying, 'Roz, have a date with Ivor.'

An odd thing had happened at the end of the evening when Ivor went out to get the car while she collected her coat. She came to the front door and stood there for a few minutes with other people who were saying goodbye to the Harveys and waiting, like Daphne, for lifts to be organised. Then, hoiking up her dress because of the mud, she started off down the drive to look for Ivor in the road. As she spotted his little green car, parked out of the light beneath the trees, somebody got out of the passenger seat, slammed the door and came stumbling towards her, splashing into the puddles in her high heels. Caroline didn't see Roz. Her head was down and she was brushing her hand across her eyes.

'Were you going to take Caroline as well?' Roz asked Ivor.

'No,' he said. 'I'm taking you.'

She hadn't dared to pursue it. But well, well, well. Fancy

Caroline coming second for once in her life. No wonder she was crying.

The drive home was passing too quickly when she wished it could last for ever. She could time the few minutes left from the landmarks they were passing. The Singing Kettle Café . . . Mr Musker's farm. Acutely aware of Ivor's hands on the wheel, she was willing him to hold her hand. She put her hand on her knee then she removed it. She put it out again and took it back. She didn't know where to put it in case it seemed to be waiting there for him to hold, so she placed it on her left shoulder then experienced a wave of delicious hurt that he'd ignored it which made her cheeks fiery. She had to try to gather her wits before they reached home and he was gone for ever.

Last time he'd stopped the car and switched off the engine with an emphatic little click. He'd stretched his arm along the back of her seat and then he'd kissed her. If she said goodnight now, and got out of the car, she might never see him again. But if she sat on with him, talking and kissing, there was bound to be an almighty ranting from Ma. What if she started hammering on the window?

'Will you come in for coffee?' she asked, as they pulled up.

'Isn't it a bit late, ducky?'

'No, no, do come. We'll be quiet.'

'All right,' he answered, switching off the engine with an emphatic click. 'Thank you, Roz. I'd love to.'

She led the way into the house, into the deep-pink sitting room and went out again to put the kettle on.

'Is that you, Roz?' Mrs Welsh called out from her bed as she crossed the hall.

'Yes.'
'Don't forget to shut the big front door, dear.'
'No.'
'Put the chain on, won't you.'
'Yes.'
'Have you done that?'
'. . . um, yes . . . no . . . look, it's all right.'
'Did you have a nice time?'
'Lovely.'
'Did your dress look nice?'
'I don't know. Mrs Harvey sent her love to you.'
'What was she wearing?'
'Tiered feathers in brown and red. She looked like a fighting cock.'
'How naughty you are!' Her mother laughed happily. 'Poor Mrs Harvey. And was Anne looking nice?'
'Yes. I saw Daphne Phelps-Phillips,' she said, terrified she was going to mention Ivor any minute. 'I had to arrange a tennis game.'
'Poor Daphne. She'll be very pleased. Be certain the bathroom water-heater is switched off before you get into bed.'
'Yes, yes.'
She went into the kitchen to make the coffee. She put instant stuff into a jug and placed it on a tray with mugs and milk and sugar.
'Roz?'
She listened.
'Roz?'
'Oh shush!' she muttered under her breath then she stepped into the hall again. 'What is it?'
'What are you doing?'

'Making coffee. Would you like some?'

'Don't be making any coffee at this hour, dear. It's after two o'clock. You'll never get to sleep.'

'It's all right, Ma. You go to sleep. Night night.' She put her head round the sitting room door. 'Sorry!' she said to Ivor in a low voice, pulling a hopeless face at the ceiling in apology for her mother.

'I'm afraid we've woken her up,' he said.

'No, no, Ma always stays awake until I come in but she'll go off to sleep now.'

'Are we to keep our coats on, ducky?'

'Wait a minute, please. I'll make the room warmer.'

She went to fetch the coffee, carried it in and very quietly closed the door. She poked the fire and revived the few lifeless embers by lighting bundles of newspaper then she heaped on a lot more coal, ignoring its scarcity because she was flustered. A fierce blaze started up.

Ivor's sleepy blue eyes studied her while she was doing it. It made her wonder if she was not doing something right and that made her nervous. He looked so much at ease, expectant in some way, that she suddenly felt awkward and unnatural with him. What if she couldn't be interesting enough for him now they were alone? As she poured the coffee, she turned herself round so that he wouldn't be able to see that her hand was shaking.

'You're very far away,' he said, his mouth quirking. 'Why don't you come and sit over here?' He patted the seat on the sofa beside him.

When she moved across to be beside him, her whole arm was attacked by a shaking leaden paralysis. She couldn't raise her hand to get her mug to her mouth.

As Ivor took it from her and set it down, there was

a thump above their heads. Mrs Welsh was getting out of bed.

They looked at each other.

'Going to the lavatory,' Roz said.

But she wasn't going to the lavatory. She was coming downstairs to see what was going on. They listened to a low muffled clomping and then the door opened and Mrs Welsh put her head round it. Her hair was in pins under a pink net. She was wearing her old brown wool dressing gown and some bootlike gaily-patterned Norwegian socks. She looked damned peculiar, Roz thought.

'I thought I heard voices and I was right! Here comes the chaperone!' Her eyes slid sideways in her head in an attempt at roguishness. Her mouth was stretched but it was not in a smile. She looked at the flames roaring up the chimney with the surprised face of somebody who has bitten into something unpleasant.

Ivor stood up.

'Ma, this is Ivor Mostance.'

'How d'you do, Mrs Welsh.'

She moved into the room. 'I'm sorry, Ivor! You'll have to excuse me . . . presenting myself to you in my hair net!'

'Looking like a hen tea-cosy,' Roz said.

Her mother gave her a quick doleful glance as if to confirm that she had drunk too much. 'I wouldn't have gone up to bed if I'd known Roz was going to invite anyone to come in after the dance.'

'I must apologise,' he replied in his beguiling deep voice. 'I'm afraid we've woken you up, Mrs Welsh. I really should be going now.'

'Do sit down, Ivor,' she said, 'and drink your coffee.' With controlled mien, she moved the Queen Anne table, which had got pushed against the wall when he threw his coat on it, eclipsing her bronze bust of Shakespeare.

'May I move your coat, Ivor?' she added, moving it. Then, for Roz's benefit, she restored Shakespeare to his usual position with reproachful ceremony. When she had removed a huge lump of coal from the fire and laid it in the hearth, she sat down, Norwegian socks set squarely in front of her. Mrs Welsh prided herself upon an ability to mix with dukes and dustmen, (her way of life meant she met more of the latter), and certainly anyone in between. She could be most charming and the young liked her because she was a great laugher and took an interest in them. 'You didn't wake me. I wasn't asleep. Roz knows how alarmed I get until she's safely home. I expect I'm known as the battle-axe mother of the district.'

'Yes you are,' Roz said.

'Well, you wait until you have a family of your own, dear.' She turned to Ivor again, her gaze moving from the thick, fair, wavy hair, brushed back from a peak on the high forehead, to the bold and amorous blue eye. Mephistopheles came to Mrs Welsh's mind. 'Where do you live, Ivor?'

'I live in Old Heaton, Mrs Welsh.'

'Ohh!' she sighed, pleased with the liberal use of her name when he spoke to her, 'Old Heaton! It is the *sweetest* village . . . one of my very favourites.'

Ivor was being won over, Roz noted, relieved.

'We're in Pinetree Drive but the best part, of course, is Heaton Hill. I've got my eye on one of those old houses set back into the woodlands.'

'We nearly lived there Ma said.' Roz was sprawled in an armchair, her hair ruffled up by the cushions, and her legs splayed out so that the skirt of her evening dress was crumpling onto the carpet. She was staring dreamily at Ivor, already walking up the garden path of their home in Heaton Hill. 'My father apparently wanted that pink house with the delphinium garden.'

'It's true,' Mrs Welsh acknowledged smiling, with a demure little bow to emphasise it. She draped her dressing gown more tightly about her legs. 'My husband and I did go and look round the pink house when we were newly married — a long time, Ivor, before this one here came onto the scene,' she added, with a sidelong smile at her daughter. 'We only decided against it because I had no car of my own in those days and shopping would have been so difficult with practically no buses. Well, it would have been a nightmare, of course, as it turned out, because my husband was killed in a car crash so soon after Roz was born.'

Ivor nodded. 'She told me.'

'Yes, he was on business in Northwich. The other driver's brakes failed and he drove straight through the red light. Geoffrey died on the spot. It was an almighty shock. But you see, I think we must have been guided not to take that pink house. I'd have been marooned there with a baby, and petrol rationed. Nowadays, it's quite different. We all drive, don't we? Does your mother drive, Ivor?'

'I've christened her the Demon because she's so dangerous.'

'Oh Good Lord!' Roz said, sitting up smiling. 'We've got another demon here. Ma's had to have her brakes replaced because she's done so much driving with the handbrake on.'

Her mother laughed. 'Isn't she naughty, Ivor! Well, I am a cautious driver. Not at all like the Demon. Poor Mrs

Mostance! You know, I have a feeling that I may know the Demon by sight.'

'Yes?' said Ivor.

'Is your mother dark-haired, tall and striking-looking?' Mrs Welsh placed her palms against her cheeks. 'She has what I would call a theatrical face? Wide apart eyes and lovely high cheekbones. She looks dramatic to me.'

He gave an amused nod. 'My mother is certainly dramatic.'

'So is this one,' Roz said, nodding at her mother. 'What's more, she belongs to the Townswomen's drama group. Strapping dames of sixteen stone deliver lines like "How much longer can we last without food? We'll all be dead soon if we don't get something to eat."'

Mrs Welsh rocked forward with laughter. 'She makes fun of us, but we won the Federation Cup with that play. Now tell me, Ivor, I've seen your name Mostance on posters for Manchester Operatic outside the bakery here. Is that . . .'

'No, no, that's not my mother. In fact, that's me.'

'My word! You must have a great talent. The reputation of the Operatic Society is wonderful, I hear. A professional standard, everybody says. What's coming next? Will you be in that?'

Roz said: 'He's got the lead in *The Dancing Years*.'

'How exciting! What lovely songs Novello wrote.' She sang a few notes in her high pretty voice. 'Waltz of my heart . . .' Her mother's face was suffused with the same saintly rapture as when she'd pronounced on bad men liking good women.

'My dearest dear . . .' he responded, returning the look as if he was already in rehearsal with her.

'Such romance!' Winifred Welsh sighed. 'We've lost all that now, of course, with women getting themselves up in trousers to be like men. Nobody has any manners. But I remember *The Dancing Years*. Geoffrey and I saw it in London during the war. It ran and ran. I'll never forget that performance and the pluckiness of the people in the bombing. Roz tells me you have a very brave job yourself, Ivor . . . a pilot?'

'Navigator.'

'That sounds a clever thing to me. I'd hit all the other planes. I don't know how you manage the Air Force and all your rehearsing. We're only housewives in our little band so we rehearse in the afternoons, but it's quite a job for us finding good plays with an all-women cast.' She paused with a small self-deprecating laugh.

To her surprise, he laughed too, rather rudely she thought, and made it worse by saying 'Woe betide the poor long-suffering husbands if they don't turn up to clap.' He pushed Shakespeare aside again to put down his coffee mug. 'As you so rightly say, rehearsals have been a problem for me. I signed on for an extra stint after National Service because I wanted to fly and it has meant turning down several plum singing roles. My contract is coming to an end now so I've got some fairly rapid decisions to make about the future.'

Mrs Welsh inclined her head, highlighting a pink coxcomb in her hair. 'Would you consider the stage, Ivor?'

As they hung upon his words, he crossed his legs, folded his arms and leant back in the chair. He seemed to Roz to become bigger and to fill the room with potential stardom. 'To be honest with you, Mrs Welsh, I haven't made up my mind. I imagine I have the talent because I appear to have built up quite a following locally — with the blue rinse brigade anyway,' he added, smiling across at Roz. 'But it's a gamble. I could stay here, get a job and have a comfortable life if I continue singing as an amateur. If I turn professional, I want to go right to the top.'

Winifred Welsh stared solemnly at him and made an encouraging sound, a sort of sighing: 'Uh huh.'

'The rewards, if you make it in my world, are jolly good. My mother's always been desperately keen on the idea. Being my mother she naturally thinks I'm the bee's knees. She's a great Novello fan. Hence my name Ivor. She's very musical herself so I owe my singing success to her, I suppose. Mother teaches the piano. She's been nursing my voice along ever since I can remember.'

Mrs Welsh's eyes were closing as she sought for words. 'How intriguing,' she murmured.

'Why don't you go to bed?' Roz said.

'I'm all right, dear, thank you. Ask Ivor if he'll have more coffee.'

'I think I really ought to be going now.' This time Ivor stood up. For a few minutes he stayed chatting, clinking his money in his trouser pocket before reaching for his coat. Then he leant in from the doorway, as if suddenly in a hurry and said briskly 'Nice to meet you, Mrs Welsh, and thanks awfully for the coffee.' He tapped Shakespeare on the head with his car keys and strode out. Roz followed to see him off.

When she came in again a few minutes later, her mother was at the kitchen sink washing up the coffee things. She was shaking her head and giving incredulous gasps. 'Woooof!' she was going, apparently to herself, shutting her eyes as if she'd been kicked in the stomach.

Roz was most annoyed. 'What's all this eye rolling?'

'I was just laughing to myself. Poor Ivor. Heh, heh, heh! He's not the right one for you.'

'I'll be the judge of that. What's poor about him?'

'Poor boy, so pleased with himself, boasting away about what a following he's got, telling us his mother thinks he's the bee's knees . . . that's a very common expression. Of course, he wouldn't be saying bee's knees if he was a bit better. It's as bad as saying tickled pink. That's terribly common.'

'He didn't say he was tickled pink.'

'I know he didn't but I'm just telling you these things so you'll know them. Only someone who didn't know any better would have the cheek to tap Shakespeare on the head like that. And he pulls his mouth up in a peculiar manner, did you notice that? Somebody should tell him about it.'

'I don't know why you had to sit there in those embarrassing clothes if that's what you thought. There was no need for you to come downstairs. He must have thought you were slightly batty getting up in the middle of the night.'

'I had to get up. We don't want to be disgraced. Guard your good name. Mrs Mostance might think you were chasing Ivor.'

'Oh listen, they chase *me*. If a man doesn't make a pass at me, I know he's queer.'

'I hope you haven't let—'

'Don't be pathetic. If there is love between two people, you don't talk of chasing or guarding good names. It's a shared love, for heaven sake.' Het up, she started emphasising her words with grimaces. 'If the man—'

Her mother laughed. 'Don't copy Ivor. You'll look like Punch and Judy doing the mouth together.'

'If the man takes advantage of the woman and uses her, well . . .'

'Don't shout. I'm not deaf.'

'I want you to take this in. *If* the man does the girl down, *she's* not the one who looks stupid, *he* does. Ivor Mostance has his own reputation to . . .'

'That boy is never going to the top, you mark my words. He may have confidence, he may have technique,' (she got the good woman's face on for the punch line,) 'he'll never get to the top because he doesn't have s . . o . . u . . l.'

THREE

Ivor was still based at his camp in Yorkshire for the next few weeks but he seemed to get home fairly regularly at weekends. Although, to her chagrin, Roz had no outings with him alone, parties were made up to go racing and ice skating. They went square dancing at the Parish Hall and she even went beagling once, praying nothing would be caught (and it wasn't), because she heard he was going. Ivor always took her home himself, but once rehearsals started for *The Dancing Years*, she didn't see him at all.

'Not long now,' he'd said, 'then I'll probably be home for good.'

But after that heartening little speech she didn't hear a word from him. She didn't know whether he was back in Old Heaton yet or not. She existed from one agonising day to the next waiting for the telephone to ring.

Her mother always greeted her with a special little smile if there was a message for her when she got in from her course at Miss Straker's. 'You've had a funny phone call,' she'd say mysteriously. But it was usually Tim Benstead, who'd been bowled over by her at the Harveys' dance, and never Ivor.

Once, she shut herself in the dining room to make a

long distance call to the Brevet Club, an RAF haunt of Ivor's, in London. He'd told her it was a good place to eat steaks and drink burgundy and smooch on the postage stamp dance floor. If he did come to the phone, she planned to ring off immediately, but at least she'd know then that he was visiting Caroline who lived in South Kensington.

The man at the other end had just said he'd find out if anyone of that name was staying in the club, when her mother suddenly opened the dining room door and poked her head round it. She had to put the phone straight down.

'I hope you're not tracking down that silly boy.' Her face and voice were dourly knowing.

'I was ringing Daphne Phelps-Phillips,' she said.

In desperation she arranged tennis, and more tennis with Daphne, because her house in Hazel Grove was quite near to Ivor's. It gave her an excuse to bike back through Old Heaton and see if his MG was sitting outside the house.

The third time she pedalled down his road, carefully dolled up ready for an encounter, he actually passed her in the car, pipped his horn and pulled up to wait for her. The hood was down. He was wearing his racing trilby which he raised beautifully like Jack Buchannan. 'If a man knows how to raise his hat properly, it will take him anywhere,' Ma said.

'How's tricks?' he asked. The greeting had an odd ring — casual and hollow. He scrunched his face up in a sympathetic bedside manner as if her welfare had been much on his mind. It made her feel pathetic. The meeting was going all wrong already.

'Are you well?'

'Fine,' she answered, totally taken aback to find he was at home and had not got in touch with her.

'What are you doing out here?'

She had an uncomfortable feeling that he guessed she was spying on him. 'Playing tennis with Daphne Phelps-Phillips.' She pointed to her racquet sticking out of the bicycle basket.

'Oh yes, old Daphne. Her ankle must be better?'

'Of course.'

'Come and have a quick drink with me?' he suggested, 'Mother's out teaching.'

She didn't answer. She fiddled with her bicycle brakes in silence then she looked up resentfully. 'Why quick?'

He threw back his head with a loud, joyful laugh. 'Roz, I do love you! Make it as long as you like, ducky. Incidentally, I like your tennis dress. You look stunning in white. I'll race you to the house,' he said, starting the engine. 'It's the green one on the left . . . but perhaps you knew that.'

Ivor's house was called Ingledene. It was a smallish, green pebbledash with leaded windows. It hadn't got an inviting smell like hers of polish and flowers and fresh washing and cooking. It was very nearly dank, because of the emptiness of it. There were modern chairs in the sitting room, a grand piano and French windows leading into a sunken, bare, overgrown garden. It appeared neglected; because, she assumed, Ivor and his mother were hardly ever in it. Not like her mother who was always at home turning out cupboards and making scones.

Ivor followed her to the window and rested his arm along her shoulders. 'Not like yours, is it? No gardeners here, as you can see. Who keeps yours in such good shape?'

'Oh, that's Jennings. He regards our garden as his really because he plants what he likes and enters all our dahlias and things in the flower shows. He's so aggressively competitive that he wins all the prizes everywhere he goes. Ma's too embarrassed to go with him because he tampers with other people's entries and moves them into worse positions. She disowns him.'

'You'd be tampering along with him, wouldn't you?'

'Ivor!'

'When I look at you, Miss Welsh, I see trouble.' He moved his hand onto the back of her neck. 'Your maid is a cousin of Betty who works for the Harveys, isn't she. She's always talking about you apparently.'

'Mary went back to Ireland last year. She got married. But nobody wants to be a maid now, do they, and I can quite see why not.'

'I'm going to have a chauffeur and a housekeeper.'

'Why?'

'You tend to want, ducky, what you haven't had.'

'I don't.'

'No, but I want to go right to the top. I'm going to come back in my chauffeur-driven Rolls and buy one of those magnificent houses on Heaton Hill. My housekeeper will look after the house while I'm working. My wife, of course,' he added, smoothing his fingers into her neck, 'will be travelling with me.'

His picture of their unfolding love story didn't altogether correspond with hers. 'But don't you like privacy?'

He laughed. 'I've had quite enough privacy. I'm sick to death of privacy. I've got an agent coming to see *The Dancing Years*. I may have the chance of a professional tour if things go well. This could be it for me, ducky. I want my name in lights!' He swung her round to give her a fleeting celebatory kiss, then, seeing the expression on her face, he suddenly pulled her against him and pushed her mouth open with his tongue. 'I didn't mean to do that.' He gave her a little push away from him. 'I can't keep my hands off you.' He moved across the room as if to distance himself. 'Now, what will you have to drink?'

'May I have brandy?' she asked, wanting to impress him.

'There might be a spot left over from the Christmas pudding to go with your Sobranies. Yes, you're in luck.'

As soon as they were settled with their drinks in two chairs, a strained silence fell upon them because she felt too bemused to think of anything amusing to say.

'So what have you been doing since I last saw you?' he asked in an encouraging voice.

'Well, nothing.' She couldn't interrogate him about not telephoning when this chasm was opening between them and making her nose run. 'You know, nothing much. I can't remember.' She timed a quick sniff with the opening of her bag and put a cigarette in a long black holder.

Ivor got up to light it for her. 'I've been rehearsing all day and every day.'

'Oh.' She nodded at the piano where music was propped up. 'Is that it?'

'Yes.'

'Oh.'

'D'you want to hear?'

'Yes please.' Relieved, she sniffed again and swigged the brandy hoping it would help her to cope.

He sat at the piano and played. For ever after when she heard this song, she was to recapture the sensation of helpless limpness as she sat there listening to Ivor talking Novello's words to her — as if he was trying to tell her he loved her. It was a moment that was to ruin her life.

> *My dearest dear*
> *If I could say to you*
> *In words as clear*
> *As when I play to you*
> *You'd understand*
> *How slight the shadow that is holding us apart*
> *So take my hand*
> *I'll lead the way for you*
> *A little waiting and you'll reach my heart*

'But didn't you ring me? You must have rung me?' she whispered to him later as they lay together on the sofa. The door was closed in case Mrs Mostance surprised them by returning. 'Why didn't you tell me you were back?'

'You do delight me. You know that, don't you.'

It was growing dark but there was still enough light for her to see his expression harden or turn gentle. His eyes were wondering as he touched her. She knew he was delighted with her. Her face was pricked and raw from the kissing.

'*Why* didn't you tell me?'

He hesitated, seeking the right words. 'You're very young, Roz . . . to be honest, and I've heard from one or two sources that people have been gossiping about us. I'm not proud of myself for acting as I have with you, but I find it embarrassing to be accused of cradle snatching. I thought it might be better if we didn't see so much of each other, that's all.'

'But why?' The shock made her feel she couldn't breathe.

'Well, for one thing, I don't think Ma would approve of what we're doing now, would she?'

'I won't have a baby, will I?'

His laugh was tenderly incredulous. 'No Mummy, you won't, because I haven't got inside you yet.'

'Have you ever been all the way with anyone?'

'Yes.'

'Really?'

'Yes.'

How could she find out who this loose one was. Not Caroline?

'Would you like me to go all the way with you?'

The idea was no more to her than a distant enormity. Whatever the consequences were of doing it in the present circumstances, she was terrified of them all. 'But I . . . I actually think people ought to wait. I want to wait until I get married. Please don't do anything, will you.'

'No.' He gave an understanding nod and then he smiled. 'You can let me know if you change your mind. I don't think you'll be disappointed in me.'

A few days later he took her to have dinner and dance at a distant roadhouse, about an hour's drive away. It was called The Hartley Arms and had coloured lights twinkling in the windows. Though it was a cold night, she begged Ivor to take the hood down for the drive home. All the neighbours must have been roused by their roaring return. Certainly her mother was.

'I suppose I'd better say goodnight to you here,' he said,

stopping in the road and reaching out to draw her close to him. 'I'll be in touch.'

She twisted in her seat to look up at her mother's bedroom window and see if the light was on. It was. Mrs Welsh was at the window.

She looked most indignant. She was mouthing words as if Roz was meant to lip read. Suddenly her right arm shot out sideways like a semaphore signal and she started to make frantic beckoning movements. Come in Boat Nine. Your time is up!

'Ivor, just drive away, please,' Roz said curtly. 'She's blown it. I'm not going in now.'

FOUR

Quite unexpectedly, Winifred Welsh had a cerebral haemorrhage and she died before Roz's baby was born. She had never even suspected her daughter was pregnant. It was the last thing that would have occurred to her.

Roz didn't suspect it either. When no periods came, she assumed it was the shock of her mother's sudden death. The shock was monumental. Although they clashed, they'd been extremely close. She felt utterly bereft. Stunned, lonely and very frightened. When she eventually discovered that she was going to be having Ivor Mostance's baby in five months time, she was so astounded that the event for a little while seemed to have no reality at all. She must have gone slightly mental.

Ivor was away touring in South Africa with a company doing *Desert Song*. After his spectacular triumph in the local production of *The Dancing Years*, he'd had an offer to join a six-month tour abroad and he'd taken it. She'd had two postcards from Capetown. That was all.

She forgave him because she realised he would be fighting for a start to his professional life. She quite understood how busy he would be. When she was particularly low, she grew apprehensive that he might find people in the cast of *Desert*

Song more exciting than a suburban seventeen year old. What if he only wanted to be with actresses now? But, after all, he had liked her all along, she assured herself. She knew how much she attracted him and their baby would cement the marriage once he'd got over the initial horrific bombshell.

'What if I have a baby?' she'd asked the night they went all the way.

'If you have a baby, we'll get married,' he replied, 'but you won't have a baby because I'll come out of you in time.'

If only she knew his whereabouts she could write to tell him, but he'd be moving on anyway from place to place. She sat in the hall waiting for all three posts each day but nothing came. Perhaps, she thought, the mail service was not reliable from South Africa. Three times she rang the post office to check how long a letter usually took and if many were delayed or lost.

She hadn't told a soul about the baby. She didn't answer the telephone so people assumed she was away. She'd told them she would be, at Ma's funeral. She wore the same clothes every day and mooched about in the house, opening drawers, looking at photographs or staring out of the window. She was unable to read. Sometimes she put a record on the radiogram, and danced the charleston like a wild thing because the doctor had warned her to beware of any violent exertion, which might damage the baby. She never cooked anything or sat down to eat. She opened small cans of baked beans when she was hungry and ate out of the tin.

She was relieved that her mother was not alive to share her downfall. When she was lying awake at night, if she listened hard enough, she could hear Ma's voice talking quite distinctly to her. 'But how could you do it? You've disgraced yourself and that's all there is to it. You drove Miss Beckfield's car up and down the school park when you'd no right to, and now our name is blackened for ever more. You can never live it down, you know. I tried to do my best for you and this is how you repay me.'

Then the idea suddenly occurred to her that she could write to Ivor. His mother must know where he was. If she sent a letter to Ingledene, Mrs Mostance would surely forward it to him. *Dear Ivor* . . . she started then she took another sheet of writing paper. *My dearest dear* . . . She crumpled that. *My dear Ivor* . . . she finally wrote.

Hope Mostance telephoned. To Roz's utter horror, she had opened the letter. She didn't attempt to excuse herself or apologise. Her voice was thin, rapid and metallic, Ivor certainly didn't get his beautiful mellow speech from her and there wasn't much sign of his charm either. Her suggestion that Rosemary should call to discuss the contents of her letter was delivered with ominous briskness. It would be *convenient*, pronounced Mrs Mostance, if she could come about five when she was home from school. Her last music lesson would be over by four o'clock.

Roz dithered about what to wear. She opened her wardrobe and dumped a pile of clothes on the bed to try on. She didn't want to get this woman in more of a state by putting on the wrong clothes. She changed her mind three times and finally went in her drab-best fawn wool dress with a round plain neck and pleats. Good style, her mother had called it because it made her look like a mousy spinster. She wanted

Ivor's mother to approve of her. She was absolutely terrified.

Mrs Mostance was a big woman, she might have been a gym mistress. She did look flamboyant and theatrical and she had her hair in a pony tail. She wore dangling earrings in the day which would have put her beyond Ma's pale.

She had rather an intrusive stare as if she was searching out the truth. Being bossy and managing must have come naturally to her because she had to earn a living in a school.

'I was extremely sorry to hear of your mother's death, Rosemary,' the Demon said, passing her a cup of tea. 'It was sudden, wasn't it?'

'Yes,' Roz answered, making an almighty effort not to cry.

'I know your mother was widowed. Have you any more family – brothers and sisters?'

'No.'

'I see.' Mrs Mostance looked most concerned. Her mouth seemed to stretch and flatten. She proffered a plate of chocolate cake.

'I had godparents,' Roz explained obligingly, 'but they died. I have an aunt in New Zealand . . . I've got friends.' She wanted to add 'And I've got Ivor', but she didn't dare.

'So you're on your own?'

'Well, I'm not on my own really. When Ivor and I have our baby, we'll . . .'

'Oh, but this is not Ivor's baby. You do know that, don't you?' His mother sat up straight. Her eyes met Roz's unblinkingly as if challenging her to repeat her lie.

The young girl stammered with shock and embarrassment. 'Y . . . yes it . . .'

'No, it's not Ivor's child.'

'Yes. Yes, it is.'

But Mrs Mostance wouldn't give an inch. 'You're a very pretty girl. You must have been out with other boys.' She kept up her pained and intrusive staring as if trying to establish whether Rosemary Welsh was either mad or bad or both.

'Rosemary, I happen to know that my son has been most careful not to become emotionally involved with anyone. He has a career to think about. Well, I've always told him straight. I said to him, "Ivor, you're not going to reach the top of the tree if you spend all your time larking about and taking girls out to dinner," and he knows I'm right!' Hope Mostance spoke slowly and emphatically as if she was attempting to communicate with an imbecile. 'Rosemary dear, how well do you know Ivor?'

'Well, I think I know him very well. We've been to lots of things together. Point-to-points and dances and . . .'

'Ah yes but he's quite a bit older than you are, isn't he? I expect he must seem rather a glamorous figure to you with his singing success and being so well-known all over Manchester.' Her eyes flickered over the pleated fawn dress. 'He was brought up by me to believe that getting a girl in the family way was the worst possible behaviour for a gentleman. He would not be irresponsible, that I do know.'

Roz's head was spinning. She couldn't hear her own voice properly. 'I know. I was brought up in the same way. He said we would get married if I had a baby. I'm sorry you are getting such a shock.'

'I am getting a shock, Rosemary. A perfectly dreadful shock.' She put her glasses on her nose and plucked up the letter which was on a small table beside her. She held it up and away from her as she skimmed through it looking critical.

While she read, Roz listened to the clock ticking, wondering if she was going to faint with humiliation and distress. 'Why have you opened it?' she wanted to cry out, 'It's not for you'.

Mrs Mostance put the letter down. She was not having her life-long dream for her only son demolished as easily as this. 'My dear,' she said, quite pleasantly, patting her palm flat onto the paper, 'frankly I would not dream of sending this hot-headed outpouring of yours on to Ivor in South Africa because there is nothing to be gained by it. My son has got his very first chance of a professional tour, his whole singing career is in front of him. With a voice like his he can have the world at his feet. Do you want to spoil his life for him?'

'But what am I to do?'

'Has the doctor confirmed your pregnancy?'

'Yes.'

'Then my advice to you is to go away somewhere. You can have the child adopted and start your life afresh. Not a soul need ever know.'

'But I want to keep the baby myself.'

Ivor's mother shook her head. 'There is such a thing as abortion, you know,' she murmured, looking rather distant and challenging and allowing her voice to trail away, 'if you know the right people. That might be the best thing.'

'What d'you mean?'

'Disposal of the foetus. It's such a quick little operation. Neither here nor there. It would be all over and done with.'

'Killed, you mean. I'm not murdering it.'

His mother said nothing. The silence and the pained look spoke for her. She glanced down and let her breath out with a tired sigh as if Roz's irrational obstinacy had brought her to the end of her patience.

'I am going to marry Ivor.'

'No,' Hope Mostance said, in a quiet motherly manner, 'marriage is out of the question. It's not his child, you see. You mustn't make any more of these silly accusations about him or he might have to get a solicitor.'

At least Roz had money after her mother's death. It seemed an unbelievable amount to her then and she was astonished. Ma had been so careful, fussing about lights left on and using up leftovers when she had such a lot of it. She felt she was going to be rich enough now to do exactly what she liked for ever and ever. With the doctor's help she went away to have her baby. But when her daughter was born, she refused to hand her over to the couple waiting to adopt her.

The nurses had always tactfully called her 'Baby Welsh' or simply 'Baby' in the nursing home. Roz didn't call her anything out loud, but from the moment she saw her, she knew her name was Flora.

'Well now, we must say goodbye to Baby, mustn't we,' Sister Sanders said when the time came. 'She's going to such a lovely home, I hear. I wonder what they'll christen her.'

The young mother held out her arms and took the child.

She held the tiny waving hand in hers, the fingers already so long and slender. Ivor's fingers. 'Her name is Flora.'

'Be a good girl. Say goodbye to her then.'

But Roz only held Flora tighter and took a secret grip on the back of her daughter's nappy. 'No.'

'Come along, pet.'

'No.'

'It's too late to change your mind now, you know, and remember, you've got your own future to think about, not just your baby's.'

'It isn't too late,' Roz said, 'I'm keeping her.'

~⁓ FIVE ⁓~

Roz was pushing Flora in her pram along the front at Littlehampton. They went the same way every day down to the water and on the way back they lingered past all the shops selling postcards and buckets and spades and '*Present From Littlehampton*' china ornaments. There were balloons floating outside, kites, monkey glove-puppets and all sorts of shiny-bright cheap toys. Flora laughed and held out her arms to reach them. It cheered Roz up and she bought her a huge light red ball. She gave the child too much.

The vulgar postcards held a horrible fascination for her. So many of the jokes seemed to be about her own plight. She took one out of the rack which showed a silly-looking blonde, with a bulging stomach, standing in a doctor's surgery.

> '*I've got good news for you, Mrs Jones*'
> '*No, it's Miss Jones*'
> '*In that case, I'm afraid I've got bad news for you.*'

Sometimes she bought cards to send to people at home but then she never posted them. She couldn't face everybody talking about her. That's why she'd chosen Littlehampton because it was big, and near to London, and because she'd never heard of anybody she knew ever going there. She'd much rather have gone to somewhere familiar in Wales, like Criccieth or Aberdovey, places she'd stayed at on holiday with her mother, but she couldn't risk bumping into anybody she knew from home. She was the only person she'd ever heard of from her own existence who had had an illegitimate child. Phrases in newspaper court reports like 'intimacy took place' still made her go hot with nervousness.

She had taken a room in a big Victorian house with a view of the sea. Sea View it was called naturally enough. She was only offered the basement, so she couldn't see the water. At first the landlady, Mrs Chalmers, had been reluctant to have an irresponsible teenager with a crying baby in the house on a semi-permanent basis but then she took pity on Roz who so obviously came from a good home though she often appeared white-faced, worn-out and unhappy.

'Cheer up, Mrs Welsh!' she might call out if she was out mopping her front step as Roz passed down into the basement, 'It may never happen!' But it was quite clear to her, as it would have been to the dumbest dimwit, that 'it' already had happened.

It was, after all, autumn then and most of the holiday-makers had returned home. She was glad of the rent while she cleaned up the rest of the house after the summer lets. She could tell her new tenant was comfortably off from her erratic, recklessly expensive manner of shopping. 'I hope there won't be a stream of male visitors beating a path to this door,' she'd remarked grimly, folding her plump arms and drawing her chins into her neck. 'That sort of thing gives a house a bad name. I like all gentlemen to be out by eleven sharp.' But there seemed to be no visitors at all, male or female, and once Christobel Chalmers had gathered that she was an orphan, whose husband had probably left her, all her motherly instincts were violently aroused. She threw herself into helping the poor young mother look after her baby. 'We must put a spot of colour into those cheeks, mustn't we.'

And Flora was an engaging child. People stopped in the street to exclaim over her. She was blue-eyed, with curly hair like ripe corn, and the slow smiley charm of her father. 'Come to Nanny!' Mrs Chalmers took to cooing, stepping comfortably into the role of grandmother in her size four-and-a-half pink peeptoes, 'The poor little mite.'

She lent Roz a cookery book full of simple, wholesome recipes and she put up a second clothes-line in the garden for the baby's washing. 'Who's going to have a chocky then?' she greeted Flora if they knocked at her door. There was always a big box of Milk Tray temptingly displayed on the sideboard. One of Flora's first words was 'chocky.' She shouted it out whenever she saw Mrs Chalmers and the landlady was delighted. Thereafter, she teetered down the basement steps on her spikey heels with hearty cries of 'It's only me. It's Chocky!'

Once inside the cluttered chaotic bed-sitting room, with its tiny kitchenette attached, her eyes darted anxiously about as she chatted. Hastily assessing the general state of things, she would tweak up a dingy-looking little dress here, inspect a piece of soiled bedding there. 'I'll just freshen these up, dear,' she'd say to Roz as she departed holding them at arm's length.

Sometimes she'd listen to her playing the same gramophone records over and over again. When she'd suffered the 'RAF March Past' or 'My Dearest Dear' for perhaps the tenth time, she'd mutter to herself 'Holy Mother of God!' and invite them both upstairs to watch television in her exotically-appointed sitting room: a riot of colour with its rose-patterned wallpaper, fluffy lemon carpet and overflowing vases of mixed artificial flowers.

Roz had to her use records as her lifeline to sanity. By playing the songs Ivor had sung in *The Dancing Years*, she usually managed to revive a spark of hope about her future. Whenever she listened to those words again, while the orchestra swelled, her mood lifted with them. She could forget Mrs Mostance. She could forget Ivor had gone away and only written her two cards. She could picture him sitting at the piano playing to her;

> *My dearest dear*
> *If I could say to you*
> *In words as clear*
> *As when I play to you . . .*

She knew their love for each other was going to triumph in the end over what his mother had done to them, because Ivor had told her he loved her and she loved him back with all her heart.

Now that she had Mrs Chalmers on her side, she no longer felt so cast out and desperate, as if her life had swept right out of control. She was beginning at last to be able to enjoy Flora although she still felt exhausted all the time. Often she simply put herself to bed at the same time and lay sleepless beside her with her face and the pillow soaked with tears.

Sometimes, without warning, her heart hammered and her thoughts raced so uncontrollably that she would have to get up suddenly to ring Ivor's number in case he was at home. If anybody answered, it was always Mrs Mostance and so she plonked the receiver straight down. In her mind she composed shocking letters to her which made the awful woman reel with remorse. She went over and over their appalling interview trying to salvage something good from it, trying to find a crumb of warmth or reassurance where there'd been none. She'd been degradingly rejected as a scheming tramp who might have had a baby by anybody. *Ivor's mother — Flora's grandmother — had threatened to get a solicitor!* Some day that musical old bitch would be in her power. When she'd done her down, she might forgive her. But probably not. If Ivor wanted her to *then*, of course, she would.

He was in her thoughts day and night. She acted as if he were watching her, approving or disapproving of whatever she was doing. In her dreams she waited for him outside stage doors or met him unexpectedly in the street. Sometimes in reality she even thought she'd caught a glimpse of his old green MG disappearing round a corner in Littlehampton. Nobody knew where she was but surely he would find her? She couldn't stop herself talking about him to Mrs Chalmers. She skated round the truth, naturally, because she didn't want the landlady to guess what had actually happened.

'Ooh yes, dear, they all come here, the theatre folk,' Chocky assured her, popping a strawberry cream into her mouth and licking her fingers in an artistic manner. 'You never know, he may easily be doing one of our shows in the town during the holiday season. Mostance is his stage name, is it, I suppose? Very nice. You need to have something a wee bit more glamorous than Welsh, don't you.'

Week after week Roz scoured *The Stage* for his name and news of him. And her sleuthing paid off. The day came when she saw a small news item announcing that Ivor Mostance would be appearing as the Duke of Dorset in *Zuleika*, a musical version of *Zuleika Dobson*, at the Opera House in Buxton. Now, at last, she knew where he was. She could write to him there.

The start of the prior-to-London tour of *Zuleika* was still weeks away. While she waited in a state of deliciously increasing excitement, Roz sat writing one carefully-worded letter after another, loving, reproachful or briefly matter of fact, and then she tore them all up. Suddenly, she had a much better idea. Of course, *of course*, she must go to Buxton herself! She would stay at the Palace Hotel, where she'd once gone to a wedding with her mother, and where Ivor would probably be staying as the star of *Zuleika*. Oh, Christopher Columbus! Thank the Lord. It was all going to come right now. How she longed for him to see Flora, he'd adore her, but would it be wiser to wait until they got used to each other again before she told him anything about her existence? She would have to leave her with Mrs Chalmers.

The landlady was only too pleased to help out. 'You go, dear. Flora will be perfectly happy with her Nanna. I don't understand why that young man treated you so badly. I'm sure you don't deserve it, knowing how you love him so much, and I'd like to give him a piece of my mind. Men! The trouble they cause us. But, fair's fair, if the Duke wants to come here, I can put you two together in my beautiful big yellow room facing the front. It's all ready. That'll give you a chance to get yourselves sorted out. You tell him that. Oh yes, I've had theatre folk through my hands for years in this house. But they're not like us, are they. They're gypsies really. It makes them a bit promiscuous and that.'

'Mr Ivor Mostance?' The receptionist at the Palace Hotel, Buxton, glanced down the register. 'No. No-one of that name. Sorry

'But I thought all the singers who came to Buxton would be staying here. Can you tell me where they might be?'

'I'm afraid I can't say, Mrs Welsh. Very often the leading ones do stay at the Palace. Others may stay in digs in the area.'

So Roz filled up the hours before the show by lying on her bed finishing Max Beerbohm's story of *Zuleika Dobson*. She'd started it at home, read it all the way on the train journey, and now she had nearly come to the end of it. She sighed with satisfaction as she set the book aside to start getting dressed. Ivor, an erstwhile Rhett Butler, was now the Duke of Dorset.

When she was ready, she strolled round to the Opera House, breathing deeply, her hands inside a brown velvet muff which had been a favourite of his. She had had nothing to eat because she was too excited to feel hungry. The setting of Buxton pleased her for their reunion. It wasn't far from all the old places she knew so well and yet its decaying crescents and old-fashioned spa atmosphere turned it into a friendly, sleeping relic of another time, tucked up into the Derbyshire hills. There was nothing to intimidate her here; except Ivor.

She was trying to keep calm, but what if the old magic between them didn't work this time? What if his mother had influenced him against her? What if Demon Mostance was here in person? 'Just be yourself,' Ma said, in her head, as she mingled in the foyer with the rest of the audience, feeling very alone without Flora.

Her seat was about eight rows back in the stalls. With a ball of nervousness rising in her throat, she watched the edges of the curtain rippling as members of the orchestra took their seats. By the time the audience was hushed and still for the overture, it was all she could do not to cry. Controlling herself made her face ache. She was completely overcome at the prospect of seeing Ivor Mostance again.

The curtain went up on nineteenth century Oxford during Eights Week and a chorus of ardent callow undergraduates in blazers and boaters, who reminded her of Tim Benstead. In this case they were all mooning after the captivating Miss Zuleika Dobson who had just arrived at the university, with her trunks of conjuring tricks, to stay with her grandfather, Warden of Judas College.

Roz hadn't long to wait before Ivor strode on as the Duke of Dorset, splendiferous scholar hero of the story who was doomed to die for her. His voice was beautiful, she'd forgotten how beautiful it was. He looked dazzling, she could have wished a bit less dazzling lest every woman in the theatre fall in love with him. She couldn't take her eyes off him. The glow of stardom was almost tangible.

'*Miss Dobson,*' the Duke said, his mouth quirking up at the corner, '*I am not versed in the tricks of wooing. I should have been more patient. But I love you so much that*

I could hardly have waited. A secret hope that you loved me too emboldened me, compelled me. You do love me. I know it. And, knowing it, I do but ask you to give yourself to me, to be my wife . . .'

She felt possessive. The words were for her because she was Zuleika. The fact that he was a bit wooden, and really neither himself nor the Duke of Dorset made her want to put her arms round him. Of course he had to convey brilliance, superciliousness and aristocracy. Woodenness might be the mode he'd chosen to tackle that.

When he took his seat, in a magnificent mulberry coat with brass buttons, at the legendary dinner of the Junta dining club, he seemed to be looking out into the audience. And when he declared, '*Put all Oxford on its guard against this woman who can love no lover,*' he stared straight at her in Row H. Roz smiled radiantly back, utterly convinced that Ivor had recognised her. She knew that look so well. ('When I look at you, Miss Welsh, I see trouble.') He knew she was there! She'd make him fall into her power again. She could not wait for *Zuleika* to end. He must have been searching for her as she'd searched for him.

When the curtain came down, and the audience started to shuffle slowly out of the theatre, she went off quickly to find a cloakroom. She put on lipstick, more coats of mascara, and little brown darts in the corners of her eyes, then she fiddled frantically with her hair. She'd look at herself, go to the door, then come back again to flatten a curl which wouldn't lie in the right direction. She had to give Ivor time to change out of his duke's costume but they might be closing the theatre by now. With her heart in her mouth and her head bent lest the breeze ruin her irresistible hair, she went outside and made her way round to the stage door. 'Darling God,' she said silently. 'Please take care of me.'

'Mr Mostance?' said the man on the door. 'Expecting you, isn't he?'

'Yes.'

'You're Miss Paul, are you?'

'My name is Rosemary Welsh.'

He glanced down at a piece of paper. 'Oh yes, sorry, my love, I've got that wrong. Caroline Paul is the lady's name I've got down here.' He winked. 'I get my instructions, you know, and I'm getting it all muddled up, aren't I. I believe Miss Paul is already with him. Mr Mostance won't want to be seeing any other visitors tonight.'

She went outside again and stood in a daze of indecision out of the light across the road. A little cluster of women, mostly middle-aged, were waiting for autographs and they pounced on 'Zuleika' as she came out. She had a slender dancer's figure, her long dark hair was splayed out over her trench coat collar and the tiny waist tugged in tight by a knotted belt.

'Where's Ivor? Is he coming? Can we have your autograph as well, please?'

'Okay. Hang on.' She put her bag down while she signed their programmes. 'His Nibs won't be long.'

'You know, we've all come in a coach from Manchester to see him,' confided a white-haired grandmother in turquoise. 'We think he's wonderful. We all enjoyed the show.'

Roz's stomach was needling. She bent over to stifle the knifing pains and almost retched. She wanted to clear off but she just couldn't move.

The stage door swung open and slammed shut as the actors came out at intervals and hurried off for a late supper in their digs. Suddenly there was an excited cry as Ivor Mostance appeared with Caroline Paul beside him.

'My faithful ladies!' He paused, smiling suavely like the Duke of Dorset, in cloak and hat, then all the fans went forward and gathered round him. He took each programme or scrap of paper in turn and signed patiently, using their backs or bags to press on and tossing his cloak aside as he wrote. His face was hidden from her by the wide brim of his hat but Roz could hear his familiar deep-throated chuckle as he asked their names, turning the brief meeting into a jokingly memorable little ceremony and making them fans for life.

Caroline waited quietly until he was ready to go, smart as ever in her short fur coat, a badger streak of white painted into her dark hair. When he'd finished, she tucked her arm into his, called out 'Night night!' and they strode off together into the damp Buxton evening, for all the world as if they were in love.

Roz trailed slowly after them, oblivious to the chattering autograph-hunters, hoping she might gather the strength to speak but not knowing what role she could possibly adopt. Betrayed mistress? Old friend from home? Delighted fan? Outraged outcast and mother of one? When they reached his old green MG, Ivor opened the passenger door for Caroline. As she got in, he leant inside to kiss her. Then the car started up, disappeared into the darkly gathering mist and was gone.

SIX

Her catastrophic trip to Buxton to see Ivor in *Zuleika* precipitated Roz's move to London. But even the sight of him with Caroline had not deadened her feelings for him. If anything, they had been twisted down deep within her into a bitter anger that would mark the beginnings of an obsession. It wasn't all over. He belonged to her. She went on making excuses for him.

Although the social climate was starting to change, she still relished the comfort of anonymity. She certainly didn't dare to go back home where every move was public. Being a virgin no longer mattered but having a baby did. Now that the worst had happened, her own attitude, always spirited, was hardening. Being in a basement room in Littlehampton was deadly. At her age she didn't want to be told that visitors had to be out by eleven o'clock even if there were no visitors. If she lived in London, she could be far more independent and adventurous. If she had to wait for Ivor, she might as well have some excitement while she was doing it. She had to move on and stop marking time.

Naturally she was hell bent on discovering how the land really lay between him and Caroline when the show reached London, so there was no time to waste. But, to her chagrin, by the opening night of *Zuleika* in Shaftesbury Avenue, he had been replaced with another singer. Ivor's name was not up in lights outside the theatre. If there was any reason given in the press, she missed it.

With him very much in mind, Roz took a flat in Mayfair. It was a most expensive place with three bedrooms and pale furry fitted carpets, in Shepherdess House, Shepherd Market, and she hired an au pair for Flora. The flat had a porter and pine everywhere which gave off a new, fresh smell and seemed the right atmosphere for a toddler. Green Park was beside them for walks.

As the house in Manchester was long since sold, and she was spending money like water — Flora was helping by running up a huge phone bill chatting to Chocky in the afternoons — she decided she ought to try and find a job. It would be a good way of meeting people as well. After three months in London she knew nobody. But she made her first friend the very day she set out, in her new sack dress from Fenwick's and Harrovian boater, to register with an employment agency.

While she was sitting there, silently sucking her pen and thinking of details to fill up a form, the door opened and an attractive older man in a bowler walked in.

'Good morning to you.' He addressed the employment agency owner in a richly fruity, far-back voice which was like a parody of all the fathers at home. He brought a newly-minted meaning to the word debonair. 'My name is Robson . . . Basil Robson. I wonder if I might take up a few minutes of your precious time?' He put his hat on her desk and sat down opposite her.

He had dropped in, he explained, on the off-chance that she might know of someone with a little extra cash to spare who would care to invest in the marriage bureau he had just started up as a sideline.

The agency woman pointed out that it was highly unlikely, dealing as she did with secretarial and clerical staff, that anybody in such an enviable state would cross her path.

'Nevertheless,' said he, 'I'd like to give you a bit more information, if I may, in case anything crops up. I'll leave you my card. I have an office manageress and factotum running it for me at the present time. I believe her to be a person of integrity.'

Just then the agency woman was called away for a moment and excused herself. Basil Robson took this opportunity to turn round in his chair and leer at Roz in the most flattering manner. In their few seconds of hasty discourse, into which he stuffed reassuring facts about himself, he was able to get across that he was ex-public school, a PR man for a big seed company and that he had a flat in the White House, Albany Street. He also managed, since she was poised to impart it, to get her telephone number before the owner of the agency reappeared to reiterate the hopelessness of his quest to find an investor from among her clients.

By the time he revealed that he had four children and had been divorced not once, but twice, Roz was already eating chicken chasseur with him at the Bistro Vino in South Kensington. He was the first divorced man she had ever met. 'Have nothing to do with Basil,' Ma was saying to her in a voice like a clarion, but the warning came too late. She took no notice.

The trouble was, he explained, the marriage business was not brisk because there were an awful lot of women

— of a certain age unfortunately — on the bureau's books but, as yet, only one man. This chap, a school master, was of all things, a self-confessed sadist. Basil had naturally felt obliged to warn any of the ladies, before they arranged a rendez-vous with him, of the sadism. To his surprise this had not proved to be an obstacle. They all professed themselves undaunted by the school master's handicap and went ahead. The man was having the time of his life.

However, he admitted, despite his high blood pressure, he had not been idle himself where the female clients were concerned. As a person of integrity, he had felt under another obligation, which was to investigate their credentials in greater depth, in order to be able to match them the more satisfactorily when other men turned up, and to keep them pleasantly occupied in the meantime. To that end, he had taken at least three of them, to date, away for the weekend — in the strictest confidence.

Basil, Roz decided, was not brainy but he was ever busy thinking up little schemes to make money and activity must count for a lot in business. She was both fascinated and repelled by the idea of his bureau. She couldn't help feeling it was all rather seedy. The people who resorted to that sort of thing must be a bit peculiar, probably housekeepers and the like. But she enjoyed hearing, in the minutest detail, about these women on the books. She was astonished that Basil, with his sleek dark, thinning hair and softly-smiling faintly caddish charm, should have such instant success with them.

He looked more attractive than he actually was. But he was exciting enough at first because London itself was so exciting. He escorted her to places and she was learning her way about. After he'd taken her to the Blue Angel, her first night club ever, she did stay the night with him with her pants on.

He wasn't pressing. She said they had to consider his blood pressure in the light of all his diversions with those slags and the lack of respect for her he might subsequently feel should anything untoward take place.

He agreed with this. He enjoyed being tantalised by a woman who kept her panties on and retained some mystery. In fact he sensed that something rather rare and special was happening between them.

Since this alien exchange only had the effect of making Roz more forlorn than ever about Ivor Mostance, when she opened her mouth again it was to talk about him, as if talking about him might help to take away the emptiness of finding herself in bed with Basil.

Now that their friendship was established, she said, she was able to tell him a secret. The reason she couldn't have anything to do with him, or anyone else, was that she was still unable to get over some absolutely terrible things which had happened to her when she was seventeen.

She described her mother's death, being pregnant and what Mrs Mostance had done, although she was careful not to mention her name. 'I'm telling you all this in confidence. You see, the situation is made more complicated because the baby's father is now a famous stage star.'

'What's his name?' Basil asked, leaning out of bed to light a cigarette.

'Basil, it's a secret. I keep telling you. He doesn't know what's happened yet.'

'I won't tell anybody about your abortion.'

'Good God, I haven't had an abortion. I've got the child.'

'Struth!' Basil exclaimed, staring at her, much moved. 'That child needs a father,' he added primly, as if he might consider taking on the role himself.

'I know Flora needs her father, that's what I'm saying, but because of his mother threatening me in the way she did, I don't know where he is. He doesn't know where I am either so he can't get in touch with me.' That wasn't altogether true of course. Faithful old Tim Benstead had written a note to her old address which was sent to her solicitor and he forwarded it to her.

'What you've got to do is get a private detective to find out where he is,' Basil stated.

Roz shivered with repugnance. 'No, no, I couldn't.'

'Well, you'll have to take him to court to establish paternity if he denies it.'

'Oh, I'm not doing that. I don't want a fearful court battle and a parcel of embarrassing scandal in the *News of the World* because he happens to be well-known. Basil, he'll know Flora's his child. I only want him to accept her because he wants to, you know. If it happens naturally, I think he will.'

'You're being a bit silly, sweetie, leaving it like this. He'd have to give you some money. My two ex-wives have fleeced me.'

'But I don't need money. I've got plenty.'

'You could invest it in my marriage bureau,' he said, not entirely jokingly, 'and come into partnership with me. I assume you're a person of integrity.'

'Mm . . . I suppose I could.'

It had crossed her mind. She'd been tempted once or twice to tell him he need look no further for a partner, but she was worried that running a business, and managing her life with

Flora, might well prove quite beyond her powers. She knew she had no discipline and she felt laden with responsibility already.

It was only after an abortive attempt to do a secretarial job, where she lasted for one day, and an unsuccessful television announcer interview — to which she'd flown late with wet hair because Flora had had a tantrum — that she realised she was probably unemployable. She took a deep breath as she became a director of the Seventh Heaven Marriage Bureau in Maddox Street, London W1, and, defying Mr Bumfrey, the family solicitor, signed away twenty thousand pounds.

From her first day at Seventh Heaven, Roz adored having her own office. Each day was an excitement to her. She could put on her Henry Heath hat and walk with ease from her flat in Shepherd Market, to her little top floor rooms knowing that Flora was playing contentedly at her nursery and would be collected and cared for by the reliable French girl, Joelle, until she arrived home. As she came up the stairs she could see the discreet brass plate winking at her:

SEVENTH HEAVEN MARRIAGE BUREAU
Consultations & Introductions
in strict confidence

Between them, she and Basil produced a pleasantly casual, friendly atmosphere in which to provide such an intimate service. Indeed, atmosphere was their strongest point. Everything else was in a bit of a muddle.

Although some of the more reserved clients were obviously taken aback at first not to find a more motherly presence, once she'd got the hang of it, Roz excelled at conducting the fairly probing interviews that were necessary, because she was good at adapting herself, like a salesman, to each person's way of thinking. She was genuinely involved and interested and could make them all feel that their search for the perfect partner was her one priority in the world. It meant, of course, that the more neurotic and demanding ones took advantage of this and stayed for ages droning on about themselves, whereas Basil was more impatient. Showing marked interest if he saw a diverting weekend in the offing, and flashing his big teeth like anything, he otherwise sat at the desk with his glasses down his nose murmuring 'Yairs . . . yairs' and 'rath*er*' and fidgeting with his papers while he advised them to lose weight or dye their hair. For a man who laughed and smiled a good deal, it was a major drawback, Roz realised, that he had no sense of humour. However, although he took two weeks off from the seed company to show her the ropes, he only popped in and out after that and she was mostly left on her own to deal with unsatisfied clients like Miss Crawshaw.

'My dear,' said Irene Crawshaw, 41, accepting a cup of tea with tight-lipped grace as she prepared to take issue with Roz over the calamitous choice for her sixth introduction, 'I want to have a serious talk with you in total confidence.'

'Oh please,' Roz replied, somewhat apprehensively, 'of course. That's what I'm here for.'

'I'm afraid I was not at all happy with Mr Roache. For a man with so little to offer, I found him surprisingly impertinent.' Since joining Seventh Heaven, she had developed a nervous eye tic which made her appear to be winking and which was becoming increasingly pronounced with each succeeding romantic debacle.

'Oh dear,' Roz said, 'I hope he didn't upset you.'

'He did upset me, as a matter of fact.'

'Well, I'm extremely sorry to hear it.'

'Yes, he was not really the type of person I was expecting to meet through a reputable bureau. After all, it's not cheap. I know he told you he was interested in botanical gardens and that was probably why you felt we had something in common, was it?'

'That and more, I had hoped.'

'There certainly wasn't more. In fact, we had a bad start when we discovered he'd worked for a friend of mine who'd given him his *congé*. We did have a reasonably interesting afternoon at Kew Gardens and he came back afterwards to have supper with me. One is taking one's life in one's hands – people tend to forget that. I don't know whether anybody else has been offended by his attitude, but he was so rude, so rejecting really, that's what got me – as if he were the arbiter of good taste. One does so hate to be *judged* and found wanting. D'you see what I mean?'

Roz nodded intently and sighed. 'I do.'

'He actually said to me "Bad luck, I*reen*" – that's what he insisted on calling me – "You've gone to a lot of trouble to please me with the meal and now I'll have to disappoint you."'

'That was a piece of utter impertinence.'

'He said "You seem to be a nice woman but we'd never get on together. Interior decoration is important to me and I'm looking for someone with feminine flair in that direction. I'd want to throw all your depressing old furniture on the nearest bonfire. I like a nicely appointed room." My dear, as if I lived in a pig sty! He was only over-looking some really rather priceless antiques which belonged to my parents. It made me very cross.'

Roz sighed again and shook her head. 'Not the right man for you.'

'I don't seem to be having much luck, do I. I think you ought to speak to Kenneth Roache about his manner and tell him to stop putting his thumb up in the air at people.'

'But you got on all right before he saw the furniture?'

'Up to a point. He'd complimented me on being vivacious but told me he thought I might be too bohemian for him. *Bohemian*!' Miss Crawshaw, a school matron, gave a short incredulous laugh, 'I ask you!'

Roz laughed too as she picked up her files and scanned a depressingly limited selection of men to find one who didn't wear a toupee or high heels and who actually intended to get married.

'Now, there's a school master – your world. I have to tell you though in the utmost confidence that he describes himself as a sadist.'

'I don't mind that. I welcome a man who's boss.'

'Or would you consider somebody a little younger than yourself – only seven years? That seems to work out well for some people. I mean, you're so full of life and perhaps a bit too much for a man as gauche as Mr Roache. I have a marital plum here called David. He's a business man – in crisps – interested in the arts.' And interested in me, she might have added. 'He's another one who asks for somebody vivacious.'

'He sounds promising.'

Roz stood up to pour boiling water into the teapot. 'What we all need is a man who thinks we're the bee's knees, don't you think?'

'Anybody who says the bee's knees is damned for ever,' said Ma.

But Miss Crawshaw laughed, with a furious volley of winking, and held out her cup for more tea. 'The bee's knees, my dear, my point *exactly!*'

Some of the disgruntled were not always so easily placated and occasionally there was quite an unpleasant upset to be sorted out.

The first time something serious happened it involved a silly girl called Sally Tilley who had been on their books for ages. Roz guessed she was going to cause a drama sooner or later because she liked to portray herself as a *femme fatale*. She suspected that she'd only registered with the bureau to get taken out and lark about. She'd probably find it difficult to get anyone with her posturing ways. She felt sure Basil had trifled with her. He'd have been impressed by the cavalier manner. She had the dated glossiness of the kept woman. Her stockings had seams, her nails were false and she'd plucked her eyebrows.

'Is Basil in, darling?'

'I'm afraid not.' Roz stubbed out her cigarette. 'Can I help?'

'Got a ciggy for me?' She picked up the packet and helped herself. 'I must speak to Basil. He's going to be livid.'

'Can't you tell me?'

'It's a bit diff, darling. This could put Basil Robson out of business. It's not something I can discuss with his secretary or anyone else.'

'He hasn't got a secretary.'

'I thought that was your job. Isn't it?'

'I'm his partner,' Roz said, enjoying the effect.

'You?' Taken aback, she blurted out, 'One of your

so-called gentlemen escorts exposed himself to me on the train to Chichester.'

'Good Lord,' Roz said, aghast. 'Who?'

'Lionel bloody Tedder.'

'Lionel Tedder . . .' Her hand shook slightly as she leafed through the files. What damage was this going to do to Seventh Heaven? 'But he's a solicitor.'

'Not for much longer.'

'But he's such a reserved man. I can't believe it.'

'Nor could I, darling. So embarrassing. I told him to put it away and see a doctor.'

Roz wished fervently that Basil was with her. 'Sally, I'm terribly sorry about this . . . I suppose you got off the train when you could and went straight home?' What if she'd told the police?

Sally laughed. 'We were going to the theatre. I was dying to see *The Way of the World* so I forgave him. I thought he might have made a misjudgement of the situation because he was so nervous.'

'Ah . . . yes, probably,' Roz agreed, dizzy with relief.

'I was quite wrong,' Sally said, 'he's a bastard. I admit I did go out with him again. We went in my car and d'you know what that man did? He tore the door handle off my little Mini!'

Roz miscalculated then. 'You must have been enjoying it, Sally,' she said, smiling.

Sally's bead-like little eyes turned to flints. 'Enjoying it?' she echoed in a sudden angry screech. 'What do you mean? To have gross indecency on the train followed by assault? Is that the accepted pattern for all dates made through Seventh Heaven?

'Listen, we'd had a few drinks at the Grenadier. When

we came out, he walked round to my side of the car as I was unlocking the door and getting in. I still had one leg in the gutter and without a word that maniac suddenly slammed the door on it. I screamed my head off!

'When he got into the passenger seat, I asked him what on earth he thought he was doing. He answered sneeringly that I'd complained about not being treated like a lady. So I punched him when we were at some traffic lights at Hyde Park Corner. He jumped out, there and then, calling me all the names under the sun. Naturally I had to go at green in all that traffic but he kept running along beside the car until he'd wrenched the door handle off.'

'It sounds to me like an accident.' Roz intended to say as little as possible until she'd spoken to Basil. 'Perhaps his coat was caught.'

'I don't give a fuck about his coat. He should have slipped out of it. It wasn't an accident . . . an accident, my foot,' she retaliated scornfully. 'No, not my foot, my right leg. See, here,' she added, pulling up her skirt, 'I've still got all these diabolical bruises. I was a fool not to go straight to the police. I hope you're going to cross that pervert off your books and somebody's got to cough up for the damage to my car.'

'I'll speak to Basil about it as soon as I possibly can,' Roz said hastily, horrified to hear a faltering step upon the stair. She stood up as the door opened and a possible new client peered nervously round the door. 'Thank you so much for telling me all about your experience. I'll be in touch, Sally.'

Roz knew that Silly Tilley would not be fobbed off as easily as that and she felt very panicky about the possible repercussions for Seventh Heaven. Keeping everybody happy was no mean feat. She found it a strain because she was so inexperienced and the problems always loomed terribly large without Basil there to bring them down to size.

He didn't come in to the office often enough and she assumed he got tired because of his blood pressure. He sometimes called in at the end of the day and slumped into a chair, smelling of whisky. She suspected he went to Soho clubs in the afternoons but entertaining customers for the seed company was part of his job.

He enjoyed hearing the gossip, and he always wanted to know in minute detail how many enquiries there had been, how many new clients had registered and how much money they had made. The petty cash box was stuffed with his IOUs. There had not been a marriage to date, (although she had had a proposal), and they had to do better than they were doing because such a lot had been spent on equipment, furnishings and printing. The rent, of course, was astronomical.

They had to discuss things together like advertising. Where to do it and what to say. Not all periodicals were prepared to carry ads for Seventh Heaven. A marriage bureau was considered a faintly seedy enterprise, not a place most respectable people wished to be caught patronising. But Roz listened and suggested and left this side of things mainly to him. Her part was to do the interviews, talk on the telephone and float about the office in bare feet looking amusingly decorative and rather daring. Basil strongly approved of that.

Roz was a born matchmaker. It gave her immense satisfaction to meddle in other people's lives and try to help them solve their problems. Sometimes it also helped to put Ivor to the back of her mind. The only trouble was that if the raw material didn't measure up, there was precious little she could do about it. The women tended to speak up if they were dissatisfied but the men merely grew more passive. Some of them were quite capable of arriving at the meeting place, taking a secret look at their prospective partner for the evening and sloping off home without saying a word. Having filled in a form indicating they were looking for a capable, serious-minded woman, if she didn't look like Bardot when she turned up, the relationship didn't get to first base.

They needed a woman to take them in hand, which Roz could do because she was not involved. She teased them, flattered them, and goaded them, and when she did that they blossomed and turned their attention to her. She occasionally had drinks with them, and a couple of the men had taken her out to dinner. But it was difficult after that, she'd learned, to send them about their business. It didn't work to mix business with pleasure.

There was one man, however, who fell into a different category. Richard Kitchener, a district officer, was home on three months leave from Fiji and hoping to go back with a wife. He had asked her to marry him the second time he saw her.

When he was in London he stayed at his club while he went to his tailor, saw plays and met old friends. He had taken to dropping in to Seventh Heaven, ostensibly to find out if anyone exciting had registered but Roz suspected it was really to see her.

He happened to come in at the very moment she needed him because she was worrying about Basil who hadn't been seen or heard of for three days. At first, she'd only wanted to speak to him about Sally Tilley and Lionel Tedder.

Now, she was beginning to wonder if anything terrible had happened. He never went right out of touch.

'Richard, I don't know what to do. I can't find Basil. His seed office say he's ill but he never answers the telephone at his flat.' How one appreciated good, straight-forward, competent men in a crisis when their disappointing lack of guile was turned suddenly into a positive asset. 'What d'you think I ought to do? You see, he's got high blood pressure. If he was feeling ill, he might have had a heart attack. Can I just tell you . . .'

'Tell me,' he said reassuringly, sitting down all ready to help in his kind manly way.

As she was explaining, the door opened and Sally Tilley stalked in looking in no mood to be trifled with. One look at Richard Kitchener, who had stood up, handsome and smiling, to meet her, and her mood instantly changed. To Roz's irritation, she sat down, draping herself invitingly in the nearest chair and looking now as if she could hardly wait to be trifled with by him.

'I fear Basil may be seriously ill,' Roz said. She turned from Sally to Richard.

'If you haven't got a key to his flat, I think we'll just have to break in,' he said.

'Yes but I don't like to leave here at the moment. In any case he may ring.'

'Well,' said Richard 'I can hardly go alone. Since I don't know him, I'd probably be arrested.'

'I'll come with you,' Sally suggested eagerly.

She might not want him herself but Sally Tilley was not having him. 'We'll get the police,' Roz said firmly. She lifted the telephone there and then, informed the police of Basil's absence and heart condition, and asked them to smash his door down.

So Richard stayed in the office while she waited to hear the outcome and Sally stayed with them, waiting for Richard.

Eventually the police rang back to say they had broken in to Basil Robson's flat and found it empty.

Basil rang himself a few minutes later to say he'd been staying with a friend in Purley for a few days because his first wife was after him for money and he was lying low.

'Oh . . . God,' Roz wailed as she put the phone down again. 'He's not at all grateful. Now, I'll have to get his door mended. I could wring his neck.'

'The feeling must be mutual, darling,' Sally said. She stood up as Richard did.

'Are you going now? Are you getting a cab? May I steal a ride, Richard? I don't know why Roz has never introduced us before, do you?'

'He's spoken for, Sally,' Roz said. 'That's why.'

SEVEN

'Are you my daddy?' Flora asked, eyeing Richard hopefully. She was holding on to the leg of his bed and swinging herself shyly in and out of view.

Roz had vouchsafed only a few incoherent nuggets of truth to surround the story of her daughter's birth in keeping with his correctness and innocence. The less he knew, she figured, the more he'd feel Flora belonged to him.

'I'd like to be your daddy, Flora,' he replied to her. 'You're my very favourite little girl, d'you know that? Why don't you bring me your *Modge & Podge* book again and I'll read it to you.'

Roz could see that marriage to Richard would be a very good thing for Flora. He'd make the most responsible, loving father. He was so jolly and masculine and even-tempered. She could imagine him administrating with monumental fairness in Fiji, striding chunkily about with his pipe in his mouth, smelling of Pears soap and devoted to his duties.

'Men like Richard Kitchener don't grow on trees,' Ma said.

Richard, for his part, was completely smitten. It was not his intention to go back to Fiji this time without a wife but, although he had no particular picture of this wife in mind, he certainly hadn't bargained for anyone as warm and wild and desirable as Roz. She was too young, too outspoken – too colourful for a colonial wife. Being so full of common sense himself, he had vaguely envisaged some equally sensible companion who would fit easily into his way of life. He had not imagined falling in love.

He took a kind of shocked delight in Roz's approach to life. The fact that she was an orphan, such a young mother and the mother of an illegitimate child, made him feel extremely protective towards her and this seemed to inspire her to more avant garde behaviour rather than less. It was as if she felt obliged to live up to his picture of her. And he made her confident enough to carry it off.

'I think I do love you, Kitchie,' she'd say hesitantly, anxious not to hurt his feelings, 'and I absolutely know I can't bear to lose you. You know, I find it awfully hard to explain to you but I just feel . . . well, really I suppose I feel . . . um *bewildered*. Now I've put money into Seventh Heaven, I've got to learn to manage things for myself for a while. D'you think Basil's all right?'

'If you've got everything properly tied up. Have you?'

'It's a partnership. I wouldn't have chosen him as my partner but I thought it was the only way to make enough to support Flora and myself and everything.'

'You do live in an extravagant manner.'

'I know. I've got to economise. I know. It's as if I've lost my balance because so much happened to me so quickly. My mother died and then I had Flora and everything that I never expected to happen in a million years happened. You see, I think I have to get used to my own existence before I can be a part of anybody else's. Can you understand that? Can you wait a bit for me?'

He tried to understand. Roz hadn't really told him anything about Flora's father but he guessed she must have been badly hurt.

'I don't want to tell you his name because then it's there for ever like a barrier between us. If I don't say it, I'm hoping one day I may forget it.' She laughed as she said it but that was her way of telling him they'd have to wait until she'd managed to blot Ivor out. But if Ivor was going to marry Caroline Paul that would settle it. She'd have to go and live in Fiji.

With that vague plan in mind, she had taken recently to ringing Daphne Phelps-Phillips in Manchester. She had told her about Flora and managed to explain her disappearance from the district in what she prayed sounded a dignified manner. Daphne, most flattered to be taken into her confidence, was easy to manipulate.

'Oh, Roz', she had said when first told, 'we all guessed you had to get away from here because of what happened to your mother. Nobody seemed to know where you were and then eventually I bumped into Tim Benstead who told me he thought you were living in London. It's not really surprising that you threw yourself into a wrong relationship with someone down there after your ma died so suddenly. You must have been utterly bereft.'

'I haven't told anyone about Flora, you know, except you.' Roz said in a later conversation.

'I know.'

'Does your mother know?'

Daphne giggled. 'Ooh no, crikey Roz! You know what she is.

'Have you gone all the way with anyone yet?' Roz had a sudden memory of Daphne in pink net at the Harveys' dance walking as if she'd been on horseback for days. An opportunity in her case for going any of the way would be a rare occasion.

'Roz, I'm not like you.'

'What d' you mean?'

'I think we look at things differently.'

'Meaning . . . ?'

'I expect I seem old-fashioned to you but I want to wait until I get married. It's just something that's important to me. Look, this is your call. We should stop. It must be costing you a fortune.'

'But it was important to me too.'

'Yes but you were always . . . oh dear, I don't know whether I ought to say this . . .'

'No, go on,' Roz said wretchedly.

'You're more reckless, aren't you. I admired you for it.'

'Is that what your mother thinks?'

'Really Roz, I don't know. She's only made odd remarks.'

'What remarks?'

'Look, don't bludgeon me. I can't tell you.'

'Why?'

'Well, you'll only be annoyed. I shouldn't have opened my big mouth.'

'Open it wider. Come on Daphne. She said I was loose, didn't she?'

'She may have said she thought you were loose. I mean you did go out with a lot of people, didn't you?'

'That's why I can't live at home,' Roz answered bitterly, exceedingly dismayed at Mrs Phelps-Phillips' pronouncement. 'I know your mother is entitled to her opinion but I can't stand that narrow, provincial middle-class outlook. It's different in London. I love it.'

'We all thought you'd stay here and marry Ivor Mostance.'

This was the moment Roz had been waiting for. Her heart started to bump. 'What's Ivor doing now?' she asked, casually as she could.

'Oh he wears frilly shirts and drives an old Daimler. I think he's in *The Merry Widow* somewhere. He's doing very well, I gather. But we all thought he would, didn't we.'

'Where does he live?'

'Hasn't he got a flat in London?'

'I've heard he's involved with Caroline Paul?'

'Yes, there is a rumour. If I bump into him, shall I give him your love?'

'Please do give him my love.' Roz kept her on the subject of Ivor as long as she could but learnt nothing more of interest because Daphne hardly knew him. 'And tell him I've got a daughter if you see him.'

'Do you want me to tell him who her father is?' Daphne was dying to know herself.

'No, no. It's too complicated. Listen, I've got to go. Flora's fallen over and hurt herself. She's yelling her head off and I must fly. I'll ring you again, Daphne. Bye.'

These chats with Daphne left her feeling unsettled and confused. She'd deliberately cut herself off from her old life but, hearing the news of all the weddings and twenty-firsts, from which she was now excluded, made her feel homesick and adrift.

'Once you get a bad name, you're done for,' Ma said. 'You can never live it down.'

Well, she was never going back to be condemned and pitied by the likes of that sanctimonious prune, Dyllis

Phelps-Phillips — parading round like a queen bee on her grandfather's ill-gotten cotton gains.

'I've got a thumping headache,' she said to Richard when he came later. 'Talking to Daphne Phelps-Phillips about my mother, and home things, always makes me feel depressed. Do you think we could just go across the road and eat at Tiddy Dolls?'

'Joelle's baby sitting, is she? Okay fine. We can do whatever you like.'

'Will you come and see Flora for a minute? She's been waiting for you to come.'

Flora was sitting up in bed. She beamed at the sight of Richard's face peeping round the door.

'Are you going to read to me? I've got my book for you.'

'Just one quick story.' He perched obediently on the edge of the bed. 'Oh no, Flora, not *Modge & Podge* again! You know every single word.'

'You said it was your favourite.'

'It's my absolute favourite. All right, off we go then. "*Emma Jones was a bit of a whiner. As her birthday came nearer, she whined more than ever before. I want a puppy . . .*"'

'Why was she whining?'

'Because she wanted a puppy.'

'Am I a whiner like Emma Jones? Am I going to get a puppy?'

'I expect you probably will get a dog some day but not tonight. And not if you whine like Emma.'

Flora laughed, delighted. 'But she got a puppy when she was whining.'

'Get on, you two!' called Roz. She came in to listen to

the last few lines of the story and tucked Flora up. She placed her panda beside her. 'Now, we won't be long. Be a good girl for Joelle and . . .'

Flora's head rose again from the pillow. 'Come and see me when you get back,' she roared at Richard. She waved goodbye with Ivor's wave.

'This is a delightful part of London to live in,' he remarked as they shut the front door and strolled out past the porter into Shepherd Market.

'I know. It's like a small, secret village. I only discovered it by chance when I first started looking. What I enjoy is the mixture of raffishness and respectability. You don't have to conform. That's where I go to eat each evening,' she said, pointing out a cheap Italian café. 'It's only seven and six.'

'But why don't you eat with Flora and Joelle?'

'Too late by the time I get home. They've eaten. I'm too tired to make anything for myself and there's never time for shopping anyway. I'll have to learn to cook properly if I'm going to look after you. I only know how to do the things that Flora likes.'

'I'm sure I should like what Flora likes.' He put his arm round her as they turned the corner into Hertford Street. 'Anyway, you won't have to cook in Fiji,' he assured her. 'There are servants. You'll need to be my hostess and you'll be jolly good at that.'

'Mm . . . d'you think.' She was only half-listening to him because she could hear Ma again. 'Don't turn him down lightly, dear.'

'Actually,' he added, as they reached the doorway to the restaurant, 'my mother could give you some good recipes. She's an excellent cook, or you could go to classes. My sister Hermione did domestic science.'

After they'd ordered and were waiting for the food to come, it was on the tip of his tongue to suggest they went down, taking Flora with them, to visit his parents in Rye. He was sure his father, an ex-army colonel, would be as captivated by Roz as he was. He wasn't so sure about his formidable mother. She might be more difficult to win over. Only the decadent or the sub-normal had children outside marriage in her experience. She'd assume Roz was a slut and start hinting that their courtship was moving too fast.

'Yes, if you want to brush up on your cookery,' he went on, 'my sister Hermione . . .'

'I don't,' Roz said smartly.

Richard's eyes opened and his jaw jutted. 'I thought you were just saying you did.'

'I loathe cooking. I was only trying to be more domesticated. Well, tell me about Hermione anyway. Where does she live?'

'About ten miles from my parents. She's older than I am by ten years and she's married to a man twenty years older than she is. Hartley runs an outlying office for the local paper in Rye. They're very involved in their church, whist drives & jam making, you know the sort of thing. They're pillars of society.' He talked on, aware that Roz had a slightly glazed expression on her face which he assumed must be concentration 'I thought we might drive down . . .' he began as their lamb was put in front of them, but got no further.

'I don't want to meet any pillars of society.' Roz said, 'It gets me down, all that stuff. But Kitch, will you teach me to drive?'

'Well Hermione has an old Ford Popular we could . . .'

'No, no, I'm going to buy a car.'

His expression was faintly pained. 'I suppose we could get you an old banger and then sell it again.'

'Oh I'm not having some shunting old wreck. I want something blissful like a sports car. I want it to have style' she said, coming to life with a naughty little smile, 'like a Daimler.' She pushed her plate aside and put a cigarette in her holder.

'You always smoke between courses.'

'I do.'

'But if we're going abroad soon . . .' Even as he spoke, feeling a spasm of illogical jealousy at the thought of Roz at the wheel of a sports car, he knew with a hopeless certainty that she was not coming to Fiji with him. It was a fantasy.

'Talking of Ford Populars,' she said, 'did I ever tell you that I was expelled from school for driving the headmistress's car down the park?'

EIGHT

Dawn was breaking at Le Touquet airport as a man and a girl came out through customs and walked towards a little four-seater plane.

They were not saying much because she was agitated and he'd been grumbling. He broke the silence between them. 'If we go back to London now,' he said, 'I'm never going to speak to you again. It's insanity.'

'I've got to get back. It's Joelle's day off. Anyway, I've got a terrible p-pain. I'll have to go to bed.'

'You could have rung Joelle and stayed in bed here.'

'No, no. I can't let her down. She has her own arrangements, you know. I can't afford to annoy her.'

'You don't mind annoying me though,' said the dentist with booming Australian geniality.

When he'd helped her into the passenger seat, he went round to the front of the plane to start the propellor.

'I need a rag to clean the windscreen,' he shouted. 'Can you throw me something down.'

'I can't see a rag . . . oh hell, do hurry,' she muttered under her breath as she delved in her bag. She opened the packet and tossed out a sanitary towel. 'Can you use that?'

He gave her a quick glance. Amusement softened his mood instantly 'Just what the doctor ordered!'

They took off and flew down low along the coastline. A man, walking his dog, looked up in surprise.

'We're not allowed by law to fly as low as this,' the pilot told her.

'Then better not do it,' she replied, wishing he'd get a move on and stop showing off.

They rose then and went up into the clouds. When they were flying over the English Channel, he switched the engine off. As the little plane dropped towards the dark surging water, he watched her face provocatively. Then he started the engine again and they nosed up steeply into the air. He did it several times to her.

'Be reasonable,' she pleaded. 'It was all on the spur of the moment, wasn't it? If I hadn't knocked your drink over in that pub, we'd never have met. I had no forward notice of our spree.'

'All right,' he relented, 'I'll forgive you. When we land at Croydon airport, we'll collect Flora and we can all spend the day together. How's your pain?'

Cornered, she looked embarrassed. 'But I've got somebody coming to lunch,' she admitted, 'I'm awfully sorry.'

'A bloke.'

'Richard's a great friend from Fiji.'

'Ah,' he said bitterly. 'So at last we get to the truth.'

The first time she drove her little red Morgan by herself was when Richard broke off their relationship. She drove home on her own without the L-plates.

Months after he'd gone back to Fiji, she was still at it. She'd taken her test once, and failed it, but as she was a good driver, she couldn't see any reason why she should be stopped by the police.

One morning she was flagged down as she roared along Park Lane at eighty-five miles an hour. Her heart was in her mouth as the constable got out and sauntered up to stand beside her open-topped car.

'D'you know what speed you were doing just now?'

'No, I don't.'

'Eighty-five in a built-up area.'

'Oh my goodness! I'm so sorry.'

In silence he looked her car over, examined the tyres and then walked round to the front of it to take her number.

'You realise your road-fund licence is out of date, do you, miss?'

'Oh . . . Lord. No I didn't, officer. I'll send off for it right away. You see, I haven't had the car long and there's such a lot to remember . . .'

'May I see your driving licence?'

'I'm afraid I haven't got it with me.'

'You have five days in which to produce it at your nearest police station plus your certificate of insurance. May I have your name and address, please miss.'

She said, 'It's Rosemary Welsh . . .' then she stopped and wiped her eye with the back of her hand. 'Oh . . . heck,' she added as if she was completely defeated.

'It's not that bad, you know.' He crouched down beside the side of the car. 'Where do you live?'

She sighed, gazing at him with wide, hurt eyes. 'Shepherdess House, Shepherd Market. You won't book me, will you. Please don't book me. I've had so many parking tickets, I don't know where to turn and now this happens. I didn't even know I was speeding because I was worrying so much about work.'

'A secretary or something, are you?'

'I run a marriage bureau. Seventh Heaven.'

'Do you indeed.' He smiled for the first time. 'Could you fix me up?'

'I could if you let me off. I won't speed again, I promise.'

'Perhaps we better have a coffee together sometime and discuss it.'

'I'd love to.'

'What's your telephone number, Rosemary?'

She told him. 'What's your name?'

'Dave Kimber. Well, I'll give you a ring then, shall I?'

'Yes, lovely.' She beamed at him. 'I'll look forward to it.'

Dave rang at four o'clock on a Sunday afternoon. Roz was still in bed, surrounded by acquaintances who had either stayed the night after last night's party or dropped in again unexpectedly during the day. She had amassed quite a circle of admiring hangers on. She'd picked them up at parties or in pubs, even on the tube. Introverted young men who called in for coffee and stayed for hours, brooding and smoking, with one thing in common; they all wanted to marry her.

She encouraged them to this point because she liked to hear then saying how they loved her, but she didn't give much thought to their mysterious bed-sitter lives when they were not with her. She didn't even always know exactly where they lived because they all seemed to move house with such frequency.

They made escorts for her, which was useful, while she

searched for the one who could successfully oust Ivor from her mind. She had a sensation sometimes of rummaging through lines of faces, as if she was sorting clothes. 'Not you . . . not you . . . well nearly . . . no, not enough . . . not yet.'

In her restless mood, her behaviour was growing wilder. Night after night for a month she'd been to Winston's Club to see the cabaret starring Danny La Rue. She danced the charleston and got into water fights, and the cycle of excitement and fatigue helped to soothe her lost, angry state.

Now her bedroom was thick with cigarette smoke, the bed was littered with newspapers and plates of half-eaten food, and all the other surfaces were strewn with cups of cold coffee and empty wine bottles. Ella Fitzgerald was singing 'Ten Cents A Dance' and she was in the middle of ringing two or three girls she knew to come round immediately and join the gathering.

Flora, still in her Mickey Mouse pyjamas, was hopefully presenting her crayons to likely victims with the plea, 'Shall we do some drawing now? Please could you draw a tiger for me?'

'Dave!' As Roz shrieked to make herself heard above the noise, she signalled for a cigarette to a solemn white-faced young man in dark glasses. 'How sweet of you to ring! How are you?' She leant forward to get a light, inhaled deeply and blew out a long floating trail of smoke. 'Yes, yes . . . I'd love to but why don't you come over here? Some ravishing women are on their way. Is it Savile Row Station? You're frightfully near, you know. Well, come if you can. If not, I'll see you at eight-thirty on Wednesday. I'm looking forward to it. Bye.'

'Another innocent fly lured into the deadly Welsh web?' enquired the pasty man sarcastically.

'Not a fly, lover, it's the police.' She called them all lover because that's what they weren't, but it could have made it seem that they were about to be.

'It's terribly serious. I've been stopped for speeding and I've only got a provisional licence.' Her tone remained high and flippant for the benefit of all those listening who needed to be kept amused. 'I was apparently doing a hundred down Park Lane. So I've got to have coffee with the constable on Wednesday. I sincerely hope the sweet little soul isn't going to book me after that.'

'We're all sweet little souls to you, aren't we?' the pale man said.

'Well, so you are. Can some sweet little soul put the kettle on for me? I'm going to make more coffee.'

'I had the impression you thought Richard Kitchener was a *very* sweet little soul?'

'He is, isn't he.'

'He's getting married, I gather.'

'Got married,' she stated briskly, irritated by the gnomish expression and desire to hurt her. 'He went back to Fiji with the most suitable wife, called Priscilla.'

'Yes, you're not really Colonial Office material, are you, Roz? Richard said he thought you were the sort of person who might suddenly throw her shoes in the air at the dinner table.'

'Oh,' she shrugged, feeling betrayed. 'Well I might do if the right moment presented itself.'

'Richard was very fond of you, wasn't he?'

'And I of him.'

'Did you want to marry him?'

'Had I wanted to, lover, I would have done,' she said, bringing the topic to a close. 'Now, don't look at me, please, I've got to get up and make the coffee. I hope nobody's going to see any ghastly sights through my nightie.'

As she picked her way among the bodies sitting on the bedroom floor, the phone rang again. Somebody picked it up and the receiver was passed to her.

'It's Daphne.'

'Daphne . . .'

'Roz?'

'Daphne! How are you?'

'Are you having a party?'

'Friends for coffee. What time is it? I'm just getting up.'

Daphne laughed. 'Roz, you're quite incorrigible!'

'What news?'

'Nothing really. I was only ringing for a chat and to see how you are. You know we talked about Ivor Mostance? Well, I met his mother and I got his address for you in case you want to get in touch with him. But, I'd better tell you another . . .'

'No, tell me now. What did the old cat say?'

'What?'

'What did his mother say? You didn't mention me, I hope.'

'No, I didn't. Listen, Roz, we can talk tomorrow. You ring when . . .'

'Don't go, Daphne. Tell me.'

'GO ON DAPHNE . . . TELL HER!' several voices shouted and a hand tweaked up the hem of Roz's nightdress.

'Can you hear these dolts? How appalling. I do apologise.'

Daphne laughed wistfully. 'I wouldn't mind a dolt. Have you got a dolt to spare for me? Sorry, Roz, yes, you must go. Ivor lives at forty-three Cornwall Gardens, London South West Seven. You do sound as if you're having fun. Are you?'

'No. I could slit my throat.'

As soon as she'd written her note to Ivor, she couldn't rest. She was on tenterhooks, awaiting his reaction. Bearing in mind that Caroline might be reading it too, all she'd said was that she would very much like to see him again.

By making herself vulnerable, so open to communal rejection, she opened up her old wounds as violently as ever. She felt as raw as if that interview with his mother had just taken place. She even worked herself up to imagining a solicitor's letter might be on its way. When her horoscope revealed that she was to receive a shock in the mail, she left the office and went home to confront it. But the post brought her nothing that day. The only shock she got was the same as every other day. Silence.

'There are always a few scum girls,' Ma reminded her, 'who can't get a boy. The boys laugh at them, of course, behind their backs.'

She tried to keep herself calm with a copy of the *I Ching*. Hour after hour she sat in her office, tossing three sixpences into the air and asking the same question. There were various pronouncements on the state of the Superior Man but whoever inhabited the book got annoyed in the end and advised her to stop asking 'what if she should fail' or she would be tied to a clump of mulberry bushes.

After three weeks of waiting and feeling exactly as if

she *was* tied to a clump of mulberry bushes, she went to find Ivor's house in South Kensington.

It was a tall house in a square. His name was not on the door and nobody answered any of the bells. As she turned away to get into the car, she saw a girl letting herself in.

'Excuse me! Wait a minute please!' Roz called to her.

The girl waited.

'I'm looking for someone called Ivor Mostance. Is this the right house?'

'Yes it is. I've seen letters on the hall table for him. I think he lives on the top floor but he must be away. Is he an actor or something?'

'Singer. You haven't any idea where he could be?'

'Sorry, I've no idea. I've only lived here for a short time. But if he's the one with the old Daimler, that's normally sitting outside when he's around.'

'D'you think I could just have a look,' Roz asked, 'and see if my letter is there?'

The girl smiled. 'Yes, do.'

It was there. 'Oh well, thanks. That's all right. He'll get it eventually. Her legs shook as she went back to the car and that familiar beat got going in her diaphragm.

Oh sod it! Sod him. Sod his mother. What a complete fool she'd been from the moment she set eyes on him. He hadn't even tried to help her when her mother died. She must be mad. It was far too late to salvage anything now. At Hyde Park Corner, she went right round and back to Cornwall Gardens to retrieve her letter. But, although she rang all the bells, nobody answered.

Flora was waiting up for her when she got home. 'You're much later than you said.'

'She wouldn't go to bed,' Joelle explained apologetically.

'Mummy's putting me to bed,' the child asserted. 'She promised.'

'So I did. Joelle, you're waiting to go off, aren't you. Thanks very much. Do go. Flora, please get undressed, sweetie-pie, I'll meet you in the bathroom in a minute.'

'Will you tell me a witch?'

Roz gave an exaggerated groan. 'All right, I'll try, if you hurry up. But it's only a lick and a promise tonight because poor mummy's got a headache.'

'You've always got a headache.'

'Yes I have . . .' she agreed absently, pushing Flora gently towards the bathroom.

'Tell me again about when Wonderwitch turned into a wasp and did sting that big fat man when he sat on top of her and squashed her?'

'Yes, but you'll have to remind me.'

She rinsed out Flora's flannel and wiped her face. 'Now ears . . . you don't want to get carrot ferns growing out of them, do you?' she said, just as Ma had said to her.

Flora chuckled. 'I've never seen a little girl with carrot ferns.'

'Well, the witch had carrot ferns. She never washed her ears.'

'Has the witch got a Kitch?'

'Oh yes, she's got a big dark kitchen with cobwebs hanging in the corners.' Roz squeezed out toothpaste on to Flora's brush. 'She makes beetle and turnip soup in a black cauldron.'

'No,' Flora said. 'You know. Has she got a Richard Kitch?'

'I'm not sure,' her mother replied, taken aback.

'You said everybody had a daddy.'

'So they do. But sometimes the daddies have to be a long way away. Richard wanted to be your daddy, didn't he, but he isn't your real daddy.'

'Is a daddy coming?'

'He'll come.'

'Will he give me piggy backs?'

'He'll be a champion at piggy backs,' Roz assured her as she tucked her up. 'You wait and see.'

When Flora piled guilt on top of all the other emotions, it nearly put paid to her. Probably she'd be able to cope with her own future but what had she done to her daughter? She went into the kitchen to make supper and sat down at the table while she thought about what to eat. An hour later, she was still there, staring into space.

She wasn't hungry. When she'd had a bath, she went straight to bed but she lay there in the same state, tense and stiff although her legs were twitching with fatigue. In the end she had to get up again and put on the same old record which always did the trick. She played it over and over again until she was comforted.

My dearest dear
If I could say to you
In words as clear
As when I play to you
You'd understand
How slight the shadow that is holding us apart
So take my hand
I'll lead the way for you
A little waiting and you'll reach my heart

She fell asleep and dreamt that a solicitor's letter arrived containing allegations from Mrs Mostance that she was extravagant, loose and unfit to be a mother. Ivor stated that he wanted Flora but not her.

'Basil, this office is a dump,' Roz said. 'You know, I think we ought to paint it and get some more impressive-looking furniture in here.'

He was looking tired and nervous. Recently he'd hurried in sometimes so distracted he almost seemed not to know where he was. It made her resentful, though she assumed he must be having a taxing time at the seed company. 'Perhaps we should just consider moving to better premises?'

That suggestion appeared to make him even more nervous. He spilt some of the whisky he was pouring out.

'Roz, have a heart! D'you know what that would cost? Anyway, it's not necessary.' He waved the hand with the drink in it. 'You've made this room look most welcoming with all your flowers and yukka plants and what not.'

'But if we've got the money for it in the bank, why not? Surely it's false economy not to have everything looking right? We need to show we're doing well. I mean I could really do with a secretary now. I'm typing all the letters myself and I can't keep pace with the filing and stuff. There's chaos in those in-and out-trays. It's only that I happen to know where to find things in the chaos. If you had to take over, you'd be thunder-struck. If you're too busy, let me speak to the bank manager . . .'

'No, no. Don't do that,' he said quickly, 'I'll deal with it.'

'See how much we can afford for a secretary.'

'You're too extravagant, Roz dear. You've said yourself you've got no head for business so leave it to me. I thought we'd agreed that I would handle that side. In any case what you're doing seems to work very well, so why rock the boat at this stage?'

'I know but I only want to . . .' The telephone rang on her desk and interrupted her. 'Seventh Heaven.'

'Hallo . . . it's Irene Crawshaw speaking.'

'How are you?'

'Fine,' she replied, actually sounding fine for once. 'Is Basil with you by any chance?'

'Yes he is. I'll put him on.' She pulled a surprised face as she handed him the receiver.

'*Irene!*' he said, putting a wealth of warmth and romantic heartiness into his greeting.

Thereafter his replies to her were brief and business-like. And obedient, thought Roz, with amusement.

'What was all that about?'

'Oh nothing.' He swung on his feet and looked a bit irritated at being interrogated. 'Something private. As a matter of fact, I'm taking her to the Cotswolds this weekend, that's all.'

'Basil . . . no. Oh, not her as well. Is that wise? Look, she's already in a state about being rejected . . . well, I know love could find a way but I do doubt it. I think you're going to upset her and then she'll come in here droning on at me.'

'I shan't upset her. She seems a very nice woman.'

'Yes but the point is your intentions are not honourable and she'll mind that. If you fall out, she'll leave us and say bad things about Seventh Heaven. Well, I'm warning you, Miss Crawshaw is not in the least happy-go-lucky.'

'Miss Crawshaw is not in her first youth, Roz dear, as you are, if you don't mind my saying so. You can rely on me to know how to handle her. Worry not.' He reached out towards the petty cash box but she was quicker. Her hand came down upon it first.

'Basil, you're not to. This box is absolutely stuffed with IOUs and you never pay them back.' She felt quite surprised at how authoritative she could be but she felt annoyed with him about everything and annoyed at life in general. 'This is a partnership, you know. Don't dismiss everything I say.'

'We'll have a talk when I get back.' He picked up his hat.

'Yes, well, don't you trifle with Irene Crawshaw,' she said as her parting shot, meaning 'And don't trifle with me either.'

'I'll give her the time of her life,' he replied, flattered and smiling, 'I might even get her to invest in Seventh Heaven. She appears to be a person of integrity.'

'Oh . . . *Christmas*. Bloody hell!' she shouted, half to herself as he went down the stairs.

On Sunday morning, a solitary one for once, the telephone rang as she was about to take Flora to the Ritz for breakfast and into Green Park afterwards.

'I need your help, Roz dear,' Basil said tersely, 'and it's extremely urgent.'

'Hullo . . . are you back? Did you have a nice time?'

'Actually we're still in bed. We've had a calamity,' he answered in the same strange stiff voice as if it was difficult to talk. 'This is monumentally embarrassing but Irene and I need your help as a matter of the utmost urgency.'

'Where are you?'

'We're at the Arbingdon Arms. It's near Stow-on-the-Wold.' His voice faded. There was muffled movement and murmuring then a dreadful groan. 'Drop everything, will you, sweetie?' he asked, speaking clearly again. 'Hire a cab to bring you to our hotel at Arbingdon Grately and then you can drive us back to London in my car. Ask for Mr and Mrs Robson, Room Six. But do hurry. We can't leave until you get here.'

'Basil, what's happened? Why are you barking at me in this peculiar voice?'

'Look, Roz, please. Don't argue with me. Be a good girl and just do what I say and don't tell anyone.'

'Has there been an accident? Are you ill?'

'I can't talk about it now but we're in very serious difficulty.'

She heard Irene Crawshaw say 'For Christ's sake!' followed by a faint cry.

'Well, I'm sorry, Basil, but I've just heard Miss Crawshaw saying 'For Christ's sake' and I am most certainly not coming all that way unless I know why I'm coming. I'll have to bring Flora with me as it is.'

He gave an appalled grunt. 'Irene is in a helluva lot of pain, Roz. Can't you try and show a little more sensitivity for once?'

'Is it a period?'

'God no.'

'You've maimed Miss Crawshaw, have you?'

'Miss Craw . . . Irene . . .' He spoke with the slow flat emphasis of desperate irritation, 'was sporting enough to allow me to . . .'

'Oh shut up,' Irene said. 'Tell her we've got stuck together. WE ARE STUCK!' she shouted tearfully down the telephone.

'Stuck?' echoed Roz incredulously, pressing her fist

hard against her mouth lest she started laughing and couldn't stop.

'Good God . . . !'

'Good *God* . . . !'

'Oh, don't be such a stupid, half-baked little twit,' Basil snapped. 'It's quite common. It's only a muscular spasm. I'm inside Miss Crawshaw and I can't get out. Headlines in the local paper could give the bureau the wrong image so we want you to pick up our clothes and pay the bill. If you bring some blankets with you, we can shuffle out to the car and lie on the back seat together until Irene lets go of me. Now are you going to do something?'

'Yes,' Roz said. 'I am.' She waited until she could control herself then she rang Stow-on-the-Wold for an ambulance.

Basil had a heart attack on the way to hospital and was transferred to the Radcliffe Infirmary, Oxford.

Roz visited him when he came out of intensive care.

'Well, old Irene did her best to put paid to me,' he observed cheerfully as soon as he saw her. 'Of course, it's penis envy, you know, which causes that sort of thing.'

'Really?'

'Oh yes, the hapless victim is trapped by the predator because she unconsciously wishes the male organ to belong to her.'

'You don't think it's nervousness?'

'Irene's certainly highly strung, I'll grant you . . . very much so. But she's a most forceful woman, with a short fuse, as they tend to have, and that combination is pretty lethal as I know to my cost with my wives. I had hoped she'd want to invest in Seventh Heaven but I don't suppose she will after this. Anyway, it's the last time I have anything to do with neurotic women like her.'

It was the last time Basil Robson had anything to do with Irene Crawshaw or, as it turned out, any of the female clients attached to the bureau. Or even the bureau itself. While he was in hospital, Roz decided to go ahead and look into the state of their finances with a view to getting herself a secretary and having the office painted. What she discovered gave her the most horrendous shock. There was not only nothing left; they were virtually bankrupt.

Gradually, she unravelled what had happened. Basil had been helping himself from their account to meet his alimony payments to his ex-wives and speculating, with conspicuous lack of success on the stock market. She had lost her entire investment, just as Mr Bumfrey, her family solicitor, had warned her she very likely might.

NINE

Of course it was quite some time before Roz's money totally ran out because she'd had a fair amount of it in the first place. She tried to run Seventh Heaven on her own but she was far too undisciplined and she hadn't enough vision or experience to run a business single-handedly. She was kind, and easy-going, and too easily side-tracked into charitable or amusing schemes which simply wasted time.

From being somewhere warm and congenial and cheap where friends turned up in their lunch hour to eat their sandwiches, her office gradually developed into a general meeting place to which people invited other people and lolled about laughing and smoking and starting unsanctioned affairs. Somehow in this atmosphere the business lines got blurred. She found it embarrassing to hand out forms for joining the bureau or to ask for enrolment fees. The days of idleness and chaos gathered momentum, her problems mounted up and she didn't know how to put a stop to what was happening.

She never had time to get the office painted. She was always tired or running late or worried about Flora. In the end there wasn't even enough money coming in for advertisements or printing. Basil Robson was meant to be paying her as much as he could afford each month but it was a rare month when he could afford anything and it was no use suing him. He had too many claims on his seed company salary as it was and he'd been told to take things quietly since his heart attack.

When there were only five spectacularly un-nubile women actually left on her books, the sadist and a lantern-jawed actor called Earl Evans who kept making a traumatic biting movement, she decided to wind everything up before she went into the gutter. Suddenly, being an employee seemed the most invitingly restful prospect in the world. She wasn't too depressed because she was an optimist and young. Life was still a fantastic adventure with Ivor all she really wanted; if not sooner then later.

She had never heard from him although she had written twice. But Daphne reported that she'd met him in the newsagent's in Old Heaton.

'I asked him if he'd seen you and he said he hadn't. When I told him about Flora, he nodded and said he'd heard but he seemed to freeze up. He kind of shut me up with that distant stare he can get and I didn't know what else to say. My boyfriend, Glyn Jones, was with me so it was a bit awkward. I just asked him what he was doing.'

'What was he doing?'

'Resting. He said he was going to Cornwall for three weeks.'

'Oh,' Roz said. 'Well, thank you.'

'Yes, Glyn and I talked it over afterwards and we both decided he reacted very oddly. He looked so frosty and disapproving . . . upset really. Perhaps he was feeling sorry for you. I mean he was very fond, wasn't he? He can't be jealous if he's going to marry Caroline. We

'. . . we . . . Flora's not Ivor's child by any chance, is she, Roz?'

'No . . .' Roz said quickly. 'Um . . . I . . . perhaps he didn't want to appear to be gossiping?'

'Mm . . . and he was never very keen on me,' Daphne replied complacently. 'He never bothered to disguise that fact. I wasn't glamorous and interesting enough for him. At least Glyn thinks I'm interesting, so somebody does!'

'Do I know this Glyn?' Roz asked, making an effort to get a grip of herself.

'He says he remembers who you are. He used to see you going riding. He works at Musker's Farm.'

'Is it serious?' Roz hoped there was no astonishment in her voice.

'Heavens yes, we're very much in love with each other,' Daphne admitted, quite naturally, then she laughed coyly. 'But I'm keeping him waiting for my answer. I think he knows already what it's going to be!'

'Daphne, I'm very very pleased. How lovely.'

'Yes, everybody seems to be getting married at the moment. You'll have to hurry up. I can't believe there isn't somebody gorgeous on the horizon.'

'I've got to get a job.'

'Poor Roz. Fancy, we all thought you were making a fortune from Seventh Heaven all this time. What bad luck that your partner double-crossed you like that. What a beast! But you do seem to have a knack of picking the wrong men.'

'Please God Professor Tunnicliffe is the right man,' Roz said to herself as she set out for Oxford for an interview to be his housekeeper.

She'd already had several hopeless interviews for posts which made her feel quite limp with boredom at the description of her duties. Anything which she might actually have enjoyed seemed to have long, vague hours and not nearly enough money attached to support her, let alone Flora.

Worrying about the child came top of her problems. After Joelle went back to France, she had never found another au pair who was nearly so reliable. It would be a great relief to be able to look after Flora herself.

Being a housekeeper, in Oxford, for a bachelor who said he was out all day and dined in college on most evenings, would surely not be arduous or beyond her powers. She was to keep house and make tea on the rare occasions when he invited post-graduates — whoever they might be. Pleasing images of herself unleashing a spellbinding Zuleika-like charm at these gatherings came to her frequently as she drove along. She hadn't expected to come across anything nearly so exciting in *The Lady*. Professor Tunnicliffe had sounded both solicitous and witty on the telephone. She felt a kind of confident thrill that they were going to get on.

After she'd parked the car, it took her several minutes to establish which of the college entrances was his. She stood for a moment gazing admiringly at all the mellowed medieval university buildings in the High Street before she went up the steps and stood at the window of the porter's lodge.

'Go straight up, please, Mrs Welsh. I'll tell Professor Tunnicliffe you're here.' As he lifted the telephone, he pointed out where she was to go. 'Take the second stone staircase on the left. The Professor's rooms are on the first floor. His name is on the door.'

Prof. H H Tunnicliffe's door had a friendly hand-written notice pinned to it reading 'Don't knock. Please walk in.' Roz let herself in to a large square room dominated by a mahogany dining table covered in orderly piles of papers, neatly labelled, and scattered books which looked new. Works for review on Locke, Hume, Frege and, one name she recognised, Aristotle. The inter-communicating door was closed but she could hear him talking heartily on the telephone in the next room.

She perched nervously on the edge of one of the dining chairs while she looked about the room. Beside her, on a notice board, there was a type-written time-table with the days divided into squares. Some of the spaces were filled in with initials, some were blank. There were entries like 'Governing Body', 'See Bursar' and there was only one for Friday — Take biscuits out of corner cupboard'. When she thought there was a silence, Roz got up and knocked on the door.

She heard Professor Tunnicliffe break off his conversation. 'Come!' he called out, impatiently, then he ran heavily to the door and threw it open.

'Oh, Mrs Welsh? Come in ... come in. I'm on the telephone. Do sit down.' He waved towards a gigantic tweedy blue sofa set across the windows and ran back down his room with bent knees, taking big steps on his heels as if he was playing Grandmother's Footsteps.

'All right, Charles. Must go. Yes, yes, yes ... I do agree, well, *en principe*, as it were. See you at the meeting on Wednesday then.' He put the phone down, took his glasses off and whirled round to greet Roz.

'Rosemary Welsh? How d'you do.' He held out his hand. He was a smallish woolly-haired man in his late fifties. 'I hope you had a good journey from London. I don't suppose the train was too crowded mid-morning? Shall we have a glass of sherry as we talk?'

'Actually,' Roz explained, 'I came by car.'

He seemed surprised. He was surprised. Surprised by her youth, her good looks, her eminent unsuitability, on the face of it, to be a housekeeper. He had never seen a woman who looked less like one. Not a worldly man, by any means, the Professor, nevertheless, had had abundant experience of the young and he had learned over the years to recognise trouble when he saw it.

'Aha, you drive, do you?' he said in his hearty encouraging way, to mute the disappointment he expected to have to deal out to her within the next few minutes. 'Now, that is always a plus.' He handed her a glass of pale sherry and sat down in an armchair beside the fireplace. 'Well, tell me what you've been doing and why you think you might like to be my housekeeper.' His eyes smiled at her rather quizzically over the top of his glasses. 'I have to warn you that I don't live in the town itself. I live in a four bedroomed semi-detached house in Headington. Most dons and their families live in North Oxford or the outlying villages and I am worried that you might find my situation a bit boring at your age and more lonely than you . . .' He broke off as his outer door was opened and someone came in. They both listened to the movements from the other room.

'Is that you, Savage?'

'Yes, Sir.'

An elderly man, wheezing loudly from emphysema, appeared in the doorway. He was carrying two plastic bags filled with shopping.

'I'll leave your shopping in the usual place, shall I?'

'Thank you, Savage.'

'I couldn't get no Persil for you, Sir.'

'Oh . . .' Professor Tunnicliffe's mouth fell open in dismay. 'Oh dear me. Did you go to Mrs Kelly's as I suggested? I am surprised. Mrs Kelly usually keeps Persil for me. Did you get anything else? No? But, Savage, d'you see, I've no soap flakes now to wash my socks. What am I to do? It's so wretchedly uncomfortable if I use a drastic detergent on them because they go stiff. I don't want to keep on having to throw them away. It's such a waste. Mrs Welsh, you're the expert, what do you recommend for washing socks?'

'Luckily, Roz remembered that her mother's stringent research into care of woollies had thrown up an outright winner. She smiled at the two men. A smile that was maternal, capable and yet, at the same time, self-effacingly seductive. 'I recommend Stergene, Professor Tunnicliffe,' she said, simply. 'It is extremely gentle and it's a liquid, you see. Sometimes a powder can clog wool, as you said yourself.' The disclosure of this homely hint, she decided afterwards, was the moment when she won him over.

'Stergene!' he repeated, terrifically impressed. He reached inside to the wallet pocket of his sports jacket and brought out an envelope. 'Stergene.' He wrote the name down on the back of it. 'How splendid.'

They smiled at each other again while he poured out more sherry.

'It must be true to say,' he went on, when his scout had left, 'that you have already had considerable experience of running a home for your little girl since your husband . . . er . . . departed. Washing for her, cooking and so forth . . . making economical appetising little meals, I expect ... I know children can be notoriously finicky eaters. I sometimes feel our college chef tries to be too ambitious. Of course, the Fellows take turns to choose the menus for a few weeks each and, quite naturally, what is one man's meat is another man's poison. It's not always something one relishes, by any means.' A beguiling vision of Mrs Welsh awaiting him in the evening at 42 Delmartin Road, full of Beatonesque wisdom, had arisen in his mind ... a delightful presence, fresh and biddable, for ever slicing and stirring delectable ingredients in his kitchen. 'Now let me tell you a little about what your duties would be if you should decide to look after me, Mrs Welsh – shall I call you Rosemary, by the way? – then you can tell me if the prospect appeals to you.'

'But I don't want to leave London,' Flora was still complaining as they turned into Delmartin Road six weeks later. 'Are we just going to stay here for a little while? I don't like this road. Please let's go home again. Oh, mum, *please*. I don't want to come to this place.'

'Sweetheart, I think you're going to like it more than you expect,' Roz replied, so tired she wanted to weep herself. 'You'll have a garden to play in and the good thing is we'll be together all the time. You said that's what you wanted.'

'I know, but I wanted it in London,' she wailed, 'not here.'

As they pulled up outside rather a humdrum pebbledash house with a circlet of rose bushes in the front garden, the front door opened and Professor Tunnicliffe emerged. 'Yes, come in ... drive right in!' He waved his arms as he ran to the gate on his heels, almost bent double.

'It's horrible,' Flora said, 'I hate it.'

'Mm . . . shush,' Roz said. But she had to agree with her.

TEN

'Is supper ready, Rosemary?' Professor Tunnicliffe tiptoed up to the door of the kitchen and peeped in, sniffing appreciatively. 'Yum yum!'

'Nearly ready.' It was her first supper for him.

'I mustn't invade your inner sanctum, must I,' he said playfully, '*divinis condimentis utere qui prorogare vitam possis hominibus*?'

'Don't speak to me in Latin, please. I gave it up.'

'I'm sorry.' He seemed a bit deflated. 'I was asking if you use celestial seasonings that enable you to prolong men's lives. I thought you might recognise our old friend Plautus, the playwright.' He started in astonishment at the confusion of cooking utensils scattered on every surface, the pile of discarded dishes in the sink. 'I *say* . . . are you doing something special? I hope you haven't gone to a great deal of trouble. What on earth are we having?'

'Mince,' Roz said, uncomfortably. It was one thing she could cook which was unlikely to go wrong and he'd said he liked nursery food. 'It won't be long.'

'Minsk?' the professor echoed, looking most puzzled. 'What is minsk?'

She reddened nervously. 'Mince,' she informed him in a

pleasantly hectoring tone, 'is . . . well, it's just minced beef. You know, *mince*.'

Professor Tunnicliffe turned away. 'A stuffing, perhaps,' he murmured, almost to himself, as he withdrew. He went into his study again and to her relief switched on the wireless.

How could she present him with this mince now? Oh Lord, how humiliating. Was he telling her it wouldn't do? He'd made her so flustered she was practically immobilised. 'What is minsk?' The stupid swine. She tasted her mince again and found it tasteless. Too much flour? She'd added stock, now there was hardly any mince at all and no more chicken cubes. While she stood panicking, she turned up the heat so the meat suddenly roared and bubbled up the sides of the pan, nearly boiling over. She leapt to the stove to lift it off and burned a corner of the tea towel in her hand. Christ Almighty! Was that his step? Oh Christmas, Ma help me. She listened, horrified. She'd have to leave this job. She couldn't cook. She couldn't give him this odd pale muck when he was expecting a gourmet dinner. She was silently wording a month's notice when she suddenly had a brain-wave. *Stuffed peppers*. Of course! She had green peppers. She had the mushrooms and carrots ready now. She had rice. Thank heaven. She'd try that. She tipped rice into hot dripping where it spat and sizzled and some grains shot off like bullets and hit the kitchen walls.

'Has there been an accident?' the Professor called out, tactfully.

'It's all right.' She stepped into spilt fat, slipped and thundered heavily against the door of the fridge.

'It's getting awfully late now, Rosemary. I think I might just have something cold on a tray in my study.'

'Coming!' she responded, going to the door of the kitchen. 'I'm just coming.'

'Ugh . . .' Flora said when she tasted her stuffed pepper. She let all the food fall out of her mouth onto her plate. 'I can't bite it.' Normally she would have been put to bed long since but Roz had allowed her to stay up so that she would have more time to spend on the preparation of her first supper for Professor Tunnicliffe.

'Mm . . . sorry, my darling. It's a botch, isn't it.' She felt infinitely cast down by her cookery failure. The peppers were still tough as footballs. She wished she didn't have to face the Professor ever again. She hated falling in his estimation.

He was reading the *Times Literary Supplement* when she went in to get his plate of half-eaten food. 'A good try,' he said, looking at her penetratingly over the top of his spectacles, 'I think the peppers could have done with a bit longer in the oven, I have to say.'

When she'd cleared up, Roz couldn't get to sleep. And when she did she dreamt of being trapped and Flora lost and Professor Tunnicliffe in his navy nightshirt telling Mrs Mostance that he wished to dispense with her services as a housekeeper because she did the washing up in Blue Grass toilet water.

He did not dine at home after that. On Fridays he was very late because he stayed on to play bridge and even on Sundays he ate in college after Evensong in the chapel. He enjoyed the services, he told Roz, although he did not believe in God. Nobody in Oxford had believed in God for years, he said. Interestingly, people's faith had come full circle. In the fourth century all the intelligent people believed in God and the morons didn't. In the twentieth century the situation was reversed.

'That makes me a moron then,' Roz replied.

He laughed happily at that. 'I'll take you to a service at Magdalen one evening,' he promised. 'The music is jolly good.'

To make up for her deficiences as a cook, Roz worked hard in the house, washing and ironing, and was careful to get his shopping right. Little daily rituals were developing. Professor Tunnicliffe sang and talked to himself in his bath before putting on a fresh shirt and fresh underclothes and coming down each morning at the same time to the same breakfast. He had a glass of freshly-squeezed orange juice, a meticulously-timed boiled egg, toast and marmalade and Earl Grey tea. She made his table look pleasant with tiny pots of flowers and laid *The Times*, smoothed neatly, beside his plate. She greeted him looking as prettily motherly as Mrs Darling in an absurdly frilly tea shop apron which showed off her waist.

She kept Flora out of his way as much as possible but he did not make her feel the child was a nuisance. He always stopped to have a word with her, encouraged her with her writing and praised any drawing she was doing. He was really most tolerant with her and Hugh Tunnicliffe, Roz was learning, was not a tolerant man. He could be impatient, arrogant and intimidating. He had a dreadful deadpan expression which signified boredom and he was aggressive towards his neighbours, although he didn't really know them, frequently imagining he'd been slighted by these inoffensive people who were actually terrified of him. She had seen him in the garden muttering to himself and shaking his fist. When she stayed too long talking over the hedge to one of the wives, she could see him silhouetted behind the net curtain and hear him gasping rudely at the banality, she supposed, and the length of the conversation. But, as long as people didn't either cross him or bore him, all was well and he was charming.

'Being in somebody else's house is very peculiar, I can tell you,' she told Daphne when she rang. 'It's all a bit unreal, I suppose, because I can't be myself but I'll have to try and get used to his pernickety ways. It makes me homesick but Flora likes it. She's at a splendid little school where she's made friends already. She was the one who didn't want to come to Oxford and now she's perfectly happy here.'

'Would Flora like to be one of my bridesmaids?' Daphne asked. 'I was going to ask *you*, Roz, but I don't suppose you'd want to, would you?'

Roz laughed. 'Ooh no, thank you. There are limits! I don't think I could get into all that, could I . . . really? De-flowered bridesmaid and single mother of one. I don't mind skulking in the background while Flora does her stuff. She'll be absolutely thrilled. It is kind of you to ask her.'

'Glyn's brother has a daughter of the same age. I've asked Cheryl too.'

As Daphne chatted on about her plans, Roz listened to her, already worrying about the wedding. She certainly wanted to go home again because she was lonely but the timing was so unfortunate. Now that she was virtually penniless she didn't know whether she'd be able to cope with the expense of the trip, let alone raise the cash for a wedding present for Daphne.

'We'll probably have the reception in a marquee because three hundred are coming. Caroline's coming, of course, so I expect she might bring Ivor Most . . .'

'Ivor?'

'I thought you'd be pleased.'

'Yes.' Oh no. Good God.

'Tim Benstead's getting an invitation but I don't know whether he'll come. He's at Oxford now, Roz. I expect you'll bump into him.'

'I hope I do,' Roz said, 'I don't know a soul.'

It was perhaps for this reason, she thought, that Professor Tunnicliffe invited her to a dinner at his college.

'What shall I wear?' she asked him the day before.

'Ah, now, Rosemary, yes, let me think about this ... er something on the lines of the infamous little black dress would be deemed appropriate, I imagine. You ladies always seem to have such serviceable garments tucked away in your wardrobes. It isn't a strictly formal occasion but the wives do dress up a bit, I have to say. It's one of the rare evenings when Fellows can bring their wives and some of them will have invited guests as well. You will be my guest.'

'I'm most excited,' she said. 'Thank you very much.'

She'd arranged for Flora to stay the night at the home of a school friend which meant she had more time to spend on her dressing and her hair. She only intended to aim at creating a modest stir in a straight silky red dress with a fringe of Twenties style pleats and a plunging V-neck. She tried on several necklaces but finally chose long black beads because of her strappy black shoes, black fishnet stockings and fantastic jet cigarette holder. The general effect, she felt, was long and lean and definitely fairly arresting.

Professor Tunnicliffe looked rather startled as she came down the stairs. He stepped back, drawing his breath loudly down his throat. 'Dear me . . . you do look . . . er . . . nice,' he said, almost accusingly.

He seemed more reserved than usual, as he drove her in to Oxford, as if he had something to say to her but couldn't bring himself to say it. She sensed he objected to her boldness. Maybe he felt she'd pulled a fast one on him by dressing up.

'Nobody at tonight's dinner will believe that this siren in scarlet is my housekeeper.' He added a dry little woof that passed for a laugh.

Silently, Roz hoped he wasn't going to tell them. She didn't want to admit she was a housekeeper. It made her feel foolish to be taking silly little orders about boiling eggs when she'd been used to running her own business. But she'd never dared to tell Professor Tunnicliffe about her marriage bureau. She knew that wouldn't go down well. He'd invented his own picture of her as an early bride, straight from the schoolroom, half-educated and totally innocent. Oh bloody hell! Sod it! Sometimes she'd get such waves of rage about Basil Robson and the money and Mrs Mostance, that villainous, old bitch. It was so galling to have to mealy mouth over everything in her life in order to hold on to this tinpot job when she'd been catapulted into this penniless mess by them. Done down by her, by Ivor and by Basil. It was their fault she was a housekeeper. Well, one day they'd be sorry because from now on she'd be the one who was doing any doing down. And she'd be doing plenty. How was she to sit at the dinner table tonight and tell people her daughter was illegitimate? She'd have to go on pretending she was an abandoned wife. Broken marriages, according to Professor Tunnicliffe, were strongly disapproved of in Oxford as undermining to the stability of university life, so her unmarried state would only sound worse still. She'd be an outcast here as she would have been in Manchester. And she needed to make friends.

She spoke to break the silence at the roundabout before Magdalen Bridge. 'Ah, I see where we are now.' She hoped he'd be impressed that she was bothering to learn one college building from another. 'Magdalen, Queen's, All Soul's, Univ,' she recited. Tim Benstead was at Trinity, Daphne had told her. 'People from home, you know, went to Trinity, on the whole.'

'That's where the Hearties go.'

'It's funny, isn't it. All the men from home came to Oxford apparently. I've only heard of one person I went to dances with who went somewhere else and that was Cambridge.'

'I'm going to turn into that lane on the right,' Professor Tunnicliffe crunched the gears as he changed down and swerved sideways narrowly missing two cylists. 'Dolts!' He pipped the horn. 'Rosemary, in a second, I'll ask you to jump out, if you would be so kind, to unlock the gate for me. Can you be ready for that?'

'Right.'

There was a second gate to be negotiated beside the Master's Lodge. Roz teetered about on her high heels, fumbling ineptly with the lock, while the Professor gasped and gesticulated in the car, then he shot past her and parked in a courtyard, bordered by garages, which was already filling up with cars.

'This way.' He ushered her into a beautifully tended walled garden.

'Oh, how lovely!'

'It is rather impressive, isn't it,' he agreed, 'It generally looks its best at this time of year. Our gardener takes a great pride in the roses.' He paused to allow her to admire them before striding on again. 'Now, we'll go up to my room first, Rosemary, if you don't mind. I need to collect my gown before we go in to dinner and I'd like to cast my eye over the post.'

As he led the way up the stone staircase, a door opened opposite his and a tall, thin undergraduate with elbow patches and a naughty, haughty, horsey face, stood aside to let them pass. Roz's eyes met his as she smiled her thanks and she was suddenly overwhelmed by a surge of excited longing for her old free, larking London existence. She didn't want a stately evening with Prof Tunnicliffe. She wanted to be off down the stairs with that gorgeous gangling horse-faced plum.

As she sat waiting on the big blue tweedy sofa, she looked about as she had not had a chance to do at her interview. It was not an unfriendly room. It had windows running almost the length of it and bookshelves from floor to ceiling at either end. Thousands of books. And there was a sweet little stepladder to reach the top ones.

If it was a bit too clumpingly masculine, with some inartistically clashing colours, it was, like Professor Tunnicliffe himself, well stocked and efficiently maintained by Savage. Like him, and his house in Headington, it was quite touching in its spartan lack of adornment but hardly invited anyone to take the liberty of sinking into cosiness.

'Well, come along then,' he said, tossing the last letter onto a pile on his desk and glancing doubtfully at her crossed legs and the expansive revelation of black fishnet. 'We'd better go. We oughtn't to be late.' He took his gown from a hook on the back of the door as they went out and shrugged himself into it. 'We all gather first for a glass of sherry.'

A roar of echoing noise, clatter and chatter from the already seated undergraduates, greeted the Ladies' Evening guests as they approached the dining hall. Led by the Master and Lady Jerningham, the stately middle-aged procession of Fellows in their gowns and wives and guests in their discreetly frumpish finery, filed past long trestle tables of young men eating their Saturday night meal in hall, towards a row of servants waiting respectfully at attention. Roz sensed heads half-turning, she thought she heard a smothered snigger. Certainly there was a general rustle of surprise as she moved past them glowing like some fiery indoor firework beside curmudgeonly bachelor Hugh Tunnicliffe, renowed for his imperviousness to the more overt attractions of the female sex.

There were knocks for silence as the Master and members of the procession reached their places at High Table and at an extra table for the overflow. Then, all the undergraduates stood up while Grace was said in Latin. As everybody sat down, Roz caught sight of the naughty, horsey man down below. His eye met hers.

She was sitting between Professor Tunnicliffe and the College Dean. While soup was served, and the buzz of conversation started up again, he turned to her immediately as the Professor turned to the bishop's wife on his right. 'Martin Nightingale,' the Dean said, inclining his head rather sweetly, 'Will you have bread?'

Roz took a liking to this tall, pale, ethereal chap whose head waved atop a long neck and thin body like a benevolent sunflower on a stalk. He greeted her questions about Oxford life with the most smilingly polite considered replies as if her conversation gave him much food for thought — as indeed it likely did. Probably, like Professor Tunnicliffe, she thought hopefully, he would have no conception of the depths of her ignorance not being used to encountering the uneducated-expelled in daily life.

'I'm Professor Tunnicliffe's housekeeper,' she felt able to declare, to test his reaction, after her wine glass had been filled several times and they had passed from whitebait onto the roast beef. 'I have a child to look after.'

'Hugh is looking very well on it,' the Dean replied warmly, eyeing the low neck of her red dress which had slipped seductively sideways. 'Never better, I'd say.'

'And are a lot of people doing theology these days?' she asked.

'Not a lot. A few.'

'Pro . . . Hugh Tunnicliffe says that hardly anyone in Oxford believes in God. D'you think that's true?'

'Well, you don't have to believe in God to do it,' the Dean pointed out.

'What are they like, the undergraduates now?' She nodded her head towards the sea of talking heads sitting beneath them. 'I mean, d'you think they're seeking a more profound meaning to life? Are they bolder, can you say, than they were in the past and more adventurous or less?'

The sunflower waved to and fro. 'Less adventurous,' he replied, 'definitely.'

At that moment a brussell sprout bounced from nowhere onto Roz's plate.

'Oh . . .' she said. 'A sprout. Look!'

Martin Nightingale regarded it politely.

She stared up and down the table. 'But we haven't had sprouts. We've had beans. Where has it come from?'

His head reeled backwards on its stalk. He looked as if he'd much rather she shut up about sprouts and beans, as if it were time to distance himself from this housekeeper and talk to someone else. He was visibly fading away from her.

She didn't like to say 'One of your unadventurous students has thrown a sprout at me' so she lifted her glass in the air, and discreetly studied the tables again on the floor of the hall. That naughty horse man's head was bent over his food. All the other heads round his were bent too and none of them were talking. They were the nearest, and in a direct line. Had it been a dare? She glanced down at herself. Was the sprout aimed to drop into her V-neck? As she looked up again, the horse's eye met hers. She opened her mouth wide, speared the sprout on her fork and popped it in. His face remained the picture of innocence.

Professor Tunnicliffe had stopped talking to the bishop's wife and was staring ahead in dignified silence. Roz finished off the wine in her glass, beamed at the people opposite who seemed oblivious to any peril from flying sprouts, and turned to him, fanning her red cheeks with her napkin.

'Martin Nightingale was just saying he thinks the undergraduates at Oxford now are less adventurous than those in the past.'

'There may be something in that,' he agreed. 'Times have changed. They all want to make money these days.'

'I can see the boy who lives in the room opposite you,' she said.

'Oh really?'

'Yes, look, he's sitting on the end of that table nearest to us. Is he nice?'

His head butted with his dry gust of a laugh. '*Nice* is not an adjective to be applied to any of them, I should have thought. Insolent, yes. Sly, yes. Conceited, lazy and hysterical, these are the characteristics of the average Undergraduate which trip off the tongue. I expect he's as tiresome as the rest. He rode into the front wheel of my car the other day, not looking where he was going of course, and he was thrown off his bicycle. I had to give him a piece of my mind.'

Hopes of an introduction faded.

'Oh, what a gorgeous pudding . . . mulberry, is it?' she asked as a cream-covered concoction like a summer pudding was served for the next course.

He smiled, looking pleased. 'This is our Elizabeth David special. Could you do one for me?'

'I'd like to try. I've never done one. Does Elizabeth David make the puddings here?'

'Elizabeth David is a cookery writer,' he explained reproachfully, his jaw tensing, 'I should have thought, with your domestic aspirations, you might know her books, Rosemary.'

She gave a nervous hiccup. 'No but I'll practise this pudding, I promise. It's lovely.'

He cleared his throat. 'I've been having one or two thoughts about our life together in Delmartin Road.'

'Oh, what are they?'

'I suspect you don't find your present duties for me particularly arduous?'

'No, no,' she assured him.

'That's what I thought. You have much less to do than

you might have since I spend so much of my time in college. But my reasons for having a housekeeper are not so that I can spend more time away from my home. I want to spend less time away from it. It isn't that I wish to place upon you all the burdens of a Mistress Quickly . . .' Here he paused for laughter so she obediently laughed too.

'Didn't she say "I wash, wring, brew, bake, scour, dress meat and drink, make the beds and do all myself"?'

'Yes . . . did she?'

'You remember *The Merry Wives of Windsor?*'

She nodded, smiling encouragingly. 'What a good memory you have,' and in his prickly way he assumed she was teasing him.

'The Jerningham's married daughter, Grace, has been attending cookery classes at the Tech. Would you like to go along . . .'

'Thank you, no, you see I don't really have . . .'

'I can spare you in the afternoons. You might find the classes helpful.'

'No, no, there's no point really if I have no . . .'

'I don't mean to be critical but there's always a point, Rosemary, in learning to do things properly. I enjoy having you and Flora in the house in many ways but I don't think I want to be waiting three hours for my supper while the kitchen is smoked out! It's in your interests, I should have thought, to learn how to run a house well and it's certainly in mine!' He finished speaking with a forceful flourish as if there was no more to be said.

And she didn't dare to say any more but she was appalled at the thought of these cookery classes and most resentful. He'd said he only liked simple food so why did she have to waste her time learning disgustingly lavish dishes which neither of them wanted? She felt belittled and trapped and it wasn't possible to get out of it. She had to do what he said. She saw now why he'd invited her to this dinner. He'd decided to drop his bombshell whilst showing her the standards he was used to.

When she first came, he'd behaved as if he was lucky to have her. His pleasure seemed to over-ride any housekeeperly shortcomings. To find that this was not now the case was an unpleasant shock. She was used to doing what she liked and, in the nicest possible way, letting other people make the best of it. When one had money, that was possible. When one hadn't, she realised grimly, it wasn't.

'Well, now, Rosemary,' he said, 'in a minute we will be moving on again for dessert. Keep your napkin with you. We change places so that we all have a chance to talk to different people. I'll find somebody to look after you.'

When Lord Jerningham pushed his chair back and stood up, everybody did the same.

'Hugh . . .' A handsome ginger-haired history don with a self-effacing, bright-eyed little wife, moved towards them. Roz had already noticed him. He'd been sitting at the other end of the table. 'Will you take my wife, Hugh?' He was smiling at Roz. 'And I'll take your lady.'

To Roz's embarrassment, the Professor whirled about and spoke most stiffly to him. 'Oh, um, I, no James, no, that won't be poss . . .'

'HUGH!' boomed Lord Jerningham, 'Perhaps you would be kind enough to take Barbara, would you, and I will look after your charming young friend here whom I have not had the pleasure of meeting yet.' Diffidently, he turned to Roz with his head on one side, his lips pursed into a tiny Cupid's bow and an air of coy sweetness as if he was on the point of chucking her under the chin, to put them both at ease. Red in the face, small, bald and stout, he looked to her like John Bull.

'This is my housekeeper, Miss Welsh,' Hugh Tunnicliffe said.

'How d'you do,' he murmured, the coyness vanishing and, again, Roz had the feeling she'd done the wrong thing by not dressing in housekeeper's clothes.

'We're adjourning for dessert, Miss Welsh. Do come along.'

Hanging up their gowns, ready for the next stage of the evening, the Master and the dons, with their wives and guests, traipsed out into the cold stone passage, up a wide staircase or two, and into a splendidly panelled room with magnificent chandeliers and portraits on the walls. Everybody seated themselves round a big wide table for port and fruit and further courteous conversation.

Roz took a few grapes from a circulating dish of fruit, feeling unequal to tackling anything else. Ma had had much to say on the correct way to peel an apple but was inconveniently silent now, when most needed, perhaps as awed by the occasion as she was.

'Port, Madeira, Graves?' Lord Jerningham pushed the decanters towards her. 'Let me help you.'

She was getting tight. 'May I?' She pointed to the white wine. 'That one looks less lethal.'

Conversation with Napier Jerningham proved more difficult than she'd anticipated. Each time she started to say something, he bowed his head towards her, (it seemed to be a collective college mannerism), while he waited gravely to hear what she had to say. What she had to say, she felt too trivial to be lightly tossed at this eminent thinker.

To her observation that this was her first Oxford dinner, he replied 'The first of many, I hope,' then there was another silence and she had to begin again. Possibly he had said all he had to say. She assumed in his position he had grown weary, and discouraged small talk; or did with housekeepers, or did with her. He would be thirsting to be engaged in intellectual debate.

'Let me help you,' he said, as the port came round again. No longer was he looking as if he'd like to chuck her under the chin. He looked, she thought, as if he'd like to be talking to somebody else.

She couldn't raise the declining spirit of adventure of the undergraduates, because Professor Tunnicliffe was sitting only a few places down the table, beside Lady Jerningham, and he would hear her piping up again. She fell back on God.

'What d'you think about this . . .' she said, speaking as quietly as she could but tapping a red-nailed forefinger on the table between them to show she was raising a thoughtful topic.

Lord Jerningham bowed mutely.

'I've been hearing . . . well, actually, Hugh Tunnicliffe was telling me about the Oxford attitude to God.'

'I do beg your pardon,' said he, (the Master was a lay member of the General Synod), 'I'm slightly deaf so you'll have to speak up. You were saying that Hugh Tunnicliffe had told you something . . . about me?'

'Oh no, no . . .' she replied, flustered, wishing he'd keep his voice down, 'about Syme.'

'Syme?'

'Yes . . . you know, Syme.'

She hurried on, fearful that he was going to ask her

who Syme was, horrified that the whole table seemed to be alerted. The bishop, opposite, stopped eating a banana in order to listen the more intently. 'Professor Tunnicliffe,' she said, nodding smilingly in his direction, 'tells me that people in Oxford don't believe in God these days. I think it's most interesting, don't you, that the situation has so reversed. I mean Syme said apparently that in the fourth century all the intelligent people believed in religion and the morons didn't. Now, it's the other way round . . . only the morons believe in God. I believe . . . do you?'

'Indeed I do,' Lord Jerningham declared coldly.

She turned to the chemistry professor on her left. 'Do you believe in God?'

'I've never thought about it,' he replied pleasantly.

She found she couldn't let the matter drop – particularly with the bishop opposite. It seemed hurtful to be mentioning his subject with no attempt to draw him in.

She smiled at him while she sought for a question which would provoke some lively talk at their end of the table.

'It's very interesting, isn't it,' she called across, 'how as we've changed, God has changed with us.'

'Has God changed?' he answered cheerfully, 'I don't think so.'

'What I mean is, first people had many gods – you know how the Greek gods were of pretty poor character – then they were all rolled into one wrathful, talkative figure in the Old Testament, who was always setting fire to bushes and turning people into salt. The next thing, he's perfect but inert.'

The bishop nodded. 'God is love.'

Lord Jerningham hung in silence upon their words, while the chemistry fellow sliced a pear.

Roz said; 'Yes, but don't you think his image will change again?'

'No,' His Lordship replied. 'Jesus Christ was sent to tell us what God was like.'

'But we only need to have people dismissing the resurrection.'

'Oh that won't happen,' he declared confidently, although it had happened already to him.

Roz switched to port as she filled her glass again. She felt happier talking to this bishop who didn't know she was a housekeeper. 'But we shower him with compliments about being wise, benevolent or houseproud, anything we choose, because he's all things . . .'

'He's all things,' echoed the bishop benevolently.

She pressed on, exhilarated by her train of thought, surprising herself, among such fine minds. 'But God's most convenient virtue these days in his self-effacement, isn't it? That's all we ask. It won't be long in my opinion before he's reduced to a physics equation, which won't give offence to anyone. That's what I think.'

Lord Jerningham inclined his head again with sepulchral gravity. 'Do have an apple, Miss Welsh, before we move on for coffee.'

'I have enjoyed our little chat,' the bishop said genially.

In the Senior Common Room she was joined by Professor Tunnicliffe. He brought her a cup of coffee, introduced her to the wife of a former Labour Shadow Home Secretary, and disappeared again.

Everybody was standing up now. It made Roz rather giddy. She felt herself tilting at the Labour wife, who was small and comfortable, and she had to keep stepping backwards to keep her balance.

'Your husband was just saying . . .'

'What?' said Roz, tilting at her. 'What did you say?'

'Your husband was just saying to me . . .'

'Oh no, no, that's not my husband.' What was she thinking of?

'I'm so sorry. Which is your husband?'

A combination of drink, the roomful of husbands and this cosy woman's sympathetic expression must have unhinged her. She opened her mouth, and whatever lies she was about to utter, didn't come out. Instead she told her about Ivor.

She could hear herself droning out her life history, while the woman listened in such a concerned and motherly manner, that she couldn't stop.

'I know it's sad for Flora to grow up without her father but from what you say, Ivor doesn't sound to me as if he's worth it, surely?'

'Well, I don't know. It's kind of you to listen. Very helpful to talk about it. The point is though,' and her smile grew radiant at the thought of him, 'he is such a dazzler!'

'Not talking about me by any chance?' enquired the red-haired history don appearing at her side. 'Can I get you two anything to drink?'

With that final whisky, Roz lost her last frail link with housekeeperly decorum. Exposed and hurting from the talk of Ivor, she did what she'd learned to do to cope with it. She amused and wooed and captivated. The response was like a drug. A blanket of protective warmth. She had to have it. As Ma had lamented on occasion in the past, she forgot herself.

She read the history lecturer's hand, she drew Lady Jerningham out about her childhood. She had a raucous argument with the ex-Shadow Home Secretary about the Royal Family. Twice Professor Tunnicliffe hastened to her side to draw her away and dump her with a battle-axe.

The third time he came she took no notice. She was giving palm readings to several of the men. She had a hand in hers, and more were waiting, eagerly outstretched.

'Rosemary, come and meet Beatrice Kemp. She's a Cordon Bleu cook. She'd like to meet you.'

She half-turned to take a look at Beatrice Kemp, a monstrous figure, staring balefully across the room. Then she laughed in the Professor's face.

'Good Lord, no.'

'I beg your pardon?'

'No, no, crafty, I'm not falling for that again. She doesn't want to meet me. You just want to get rid of her.'

His eyes were gleaming behind his glasses. 'I'm afraid I don't understand you.'

Roz handed back the hand she was holding. She straightened up then she tilted alarmingly towards him and tapped him on the cheek. 'Little Hughie,' she murmured giggling. 'Sometimes you ask too much, lover.'

'You're drunk, Rosemary.' He looked absolutely livid with her. 'Would you go and get your coat, please.'

ELEVEN

'And this is my daughter, Flora,' Roz was saying to Caroline Paul as they stood together drinking champagne at Daphne Phelps-Phillips' wedding reception in a marquee on the lawn.

'Good heavens! Flora! I didn't know you were as grown up as this!' Caroline obligingly staggered backwards on her spiky heels pretending to be overcome with shock at Flora's size. 'Well, I was watching you in church. You were still as a mouse. You made the best bridesmaid ever.'

Flora beamed at her from beneath a circlet of tiny yellow flowers which peeped out from her fair curls. Over-excited, she spun about, showing off in her lemon silk dress with embroidered sash. 'I never did tread on Aunty Daphne's train so I'm going to get half a crown,' she informed her. 'Can I have it now?' she added, as an inspired afterthought, turning to her mother.

'Flora!' Roz laughed, 'You're disgracing me! I'll give you the money when we get home.' It crossed her mind with a tiny thrill of horror that if she parted with so much as a penny more at this point, they might not have enough money for the petrol back to Oxford.

'It's *so* nice to see you again,' Caroline said, tapping her arm affectionately. 'I don't know why on earth we've lost touch for so long, do you?'

So she was not thinking of Ivor as the reason, thank goodness. Roz felt extremely relieved he wasn't with her. Seeing them standing side by side during the marriage service would have taken a toll. It was bad enough, as it was, trying not to cry. 'I know, it's awful, isn't it. But time flies by and everybody gets so busy in their own existences. You see, I'm living in Oxford now.' Pleased as she was to see Caroline again, the sight of her had thrown her right off balance. She'd almost forgotten what a stunner she was. Whatever any of them did, Caroline was always going to be a jump ahead — in looks and in life.

'What are you doing in Oxford, Roz?'

'Oh, God, I've only just got there really. I've got a job helping this professor to organise his house and . . .'

'Interior decorating?'

'No, no, I'm a sort of social figure for him, you know . . . well, actually, a hostess for visiting academics and graduate students and that sort of thing,' she expounded vaguely, determined not to utter the word 'housekeeper' and mindful that whatever she did say would be passed on to Ivor. 'Flora loves it there but I'm not sure whether it's going to last long because I . . .' She half-turned, aware of another person now standing beside them, and trailed off, glad of an excuse to shut up.

'Tim! Hullo!' Caroline smiled, 'How are you?'

'Hullo Tim,' Roz echoed, thinking how sweet he looked in morning dress and remembering guiltily that she had never replied to his letter.

'How's the brain surgery?' he asked her.

'My dear,' she replied theatrically, 'I can hardly keep pace with the demand for my lobotomies.'

They all laughed. And Roz recounted her original conversation with Tim when they met at Anne Harvey's dance all those years ago.

'What are you doing now?' she asked him.

'Medicine.'

'And then?'

'A brain surgeon.'

'I do not believe you!'

'Tim . . . Tim . . . quick! Do come over here a minute. Sue wants to ask you something frightfully important!' A giggling blonde was tugging at his arm. 'Can I borrow Tim?' she begged Caroline and Roz as she dragged him away.

'See you later,' he said, grimacing over his shoulder.

'Oh,' Caroline said, 'what a pity. I like Tim Benstead.'

'Yes, I like him too.'

'And he likes you.'

'Well, you know, I haven't seen him for years either. I must say I do love coming back.'

Just then the speeches started. 'Mummay . . . mum . . . look at me!' Flora gave a shout into the silence and jumped off a chair.

'Shush sweetheart. Come here and behave yourself. No talking now.'

As Glyn's brother, Robert, began to read out the telegrams, she was overcome with a most pleasant, champagne-induced sense of well-being. Coming home had not been the appalling ordeal she had anticipated. Times had changed and even middle-class Cheshire had changed with them. They were all sleeping together now so there hadn't been embarrassment about Flora, although she was glad she'd chosen this fleeting and artificial occasion when there was only time for brief rapturous greetings with the old friends, and all the attention really belonged to Daphne on her wedding day. She'd been treated, just as she'd hoped to be, as an envied *outré* figure from the big city. She hadn't been made to feel odd, or beyond the pale or pathetic as she'd feared. In any case, Daphne Phelps-Phillips was doing something pretty odd herself in marrying a farm labourer.

He made a tiny passive figure beside her now, amiable and rosy from the raw morning winds. Roz recognised him even without his old brown cap. She remembered him because they'd always waved to each other as he drove the tractor home from Mr Musker's far flung fields. None of Glyn's guests were in morning clothes but all Daphne's were. One side of the church had come in fancy dress and the other had come in whatever they had.

'In true romantic tradition,' he said when it was the bridegroom's turn to speak, 'I fell in love with Daphne in the hay loft when she used to come to the farm to get hay for her horses. I knew she'd make me a good farmer's wife because she was no mean hand with a bale . . .' He paused, waiting for the ripple of laughter to subside and Daphne swiped at him playfully.

'I give it five years,' Caroline muttered out of the side of her mouth. 'She's going to make mincemeat of that little man.'

'It may be all right if they have a farm together,' Roz whispered back. 'A joint endeavour. He'll have the knowledge and she'll have the cash.'

She watched Daphne curiously while she was cutting the cake with Glyn. There was really no knowing about the capriciousness of love's dart if those two could form a union.

Daphne was bigger than ever. She looked older too. She might have been Glyn's mother. She was romping about, Roz thought, like some vulgar matron in a Restoration comedy. Love had made her jovial and assured, she wasn't a wall flower now.

Poor Daphne, Ma had always said, it'll be a battle for those parents of hers to get that big lump off with anyone.

'Who'd have thought Daff would beat us all to it?' Caroline remarked, carefully selecting the smallest bit of wedding cake as it was handed round.

'Well, she's looking rather nubile.'

'Nubile, Roz? No.'

The waitress bent down to Flora.

'Ooh, Flora, not the biggest piece . . . you'll be sick. Now, why don't you play with Cheryl?'

'She's really rather young for me.'

'You two bridesmaids ought to stick together. You should help to look after her. Look, there she is, over there, near her father. Go and see,' Roz said, deliberately created an abstracted aura to surround her next words to Caroline.

'I thought you were going to be the first off. In fact, I expected you'd bring Ivor with you today.'

'No, no. That's all over now, I'm afraid.'

'Over?'

'Yes.' Caroline seemed quite composed. 'It didn't work out for us.'

'I am sorry.' Praise the saints! Was it true?

'I'm sorry too,' she answered slowly as if she might still be having doubts, 'I loved that man.'

'Did you?'

'I really did.' She suddenly abandoned her cake on

a dirty plate and got out a handkerchief to wipe her hands.

'Why didn't it work? I'm amazed.'

'I suppose it was because I simply couldn't stand our way of life.'

Roz felt a dart of disappointment that the break came from her side, leaving Ivor mourning for her. 'But wasn't his theatrical life rather fun?'

'Fun for them. I always wished I was part of that myself but I was a hanger on. I had nothing to do all day except wait in the digs, which are ghastly, or sit in the dressing rooms. He wanted me to be with him or we practically never saw each other. I cannot tell you how bored I got. I had to find things to do to amuse myself in all these places like Birmingham or Newcastle, and on Sundays you're travelling again. Of course I loved the times when Ivor was out of work but he got so twitchy then about no money coming in that it made him very difficult to live with. He's got such grand ideas. He gets so impatient and depressed when things don't go right.'

'Is he heartbroken?'

She shook her head. 'No, I don't think so. I think he's found someone else. He'd never be without a woman for long. There's always a queue waiting in the wings. You know Ivor.

'I used to feel madly jealous of you at one time,' she admitted smiling, 'when I thought he liked you. I went home in tears from Anne Harvey's dance the night you danced the charleston with him. Wasn't it silly?'

Hearing Ivor described as living an ordinary life — a thing he'd never done, in her mind — was very strange. These bombshells were taking a terrible toll. It wasn't easy to respond and still sound sufficiently casual. In a minute she was going to slump to the ground. 'I haven't seen Ivor for years. Daphne used to give me news of everyone so I heard things about you from time to time. Did she tell you and Ivor that I'd had Flora?'

'His mother did. For some extraordinary reason Ivor would never talk about you. I used to pump him, of course,' she admitted, giving her infectious laugh, 'but I got *nothing*!'

'What did Mrs Mostance say?'

'Roz, you know what mothers can be like, and Hope Mostance was that with knobs on. To be honest I found her an awful pain in the neck — so fixated on her darling boy. I wasn't good enough for him, naturally

'Naturally!' Roz laughed with her. 'So what did she have to say about me?'

'Oh, she's such an old hypocrite, isn't she. She was always slipping off to this chap for dirty weekends in Sussex herself. Then they had an appalling car crash together. It was his fault apparently and she was terribly badly injured. She's crippled really, I gather, and she's had to have plastic surgery. Anyway, he's married her and they live in some little village near the Sussex coast.'

'Heavens.' Well, strike me pink! Good old God. She asked for it and now she's got it. 'Poor Ivor.'

'Yes.'

'I can imagine what she said about me.'

'Yes.'

'But tell me. Caroline, go on. I can't imagine it well enough!'

'Oh, she kept saying how shocked she was. How irresponsible of you and all that. Yes, she once announced that you'd gone to London to become a whore. We all had a terrible argument about it, starting with you and going on to other issues!'

'Very good of you to support me. Thanks. I could drop dead with annoyance. So what did she have to say about Flora's father?'

'What she actually said was that you'd been out with a lot of men and nobody knew who the father was. She always got frightfully tight-lipped on the subject as if it was a warning or something to Ivor and me. I expect she's blackening my name now. Anyway, I bet Flora's father is lovely, isn't he? Is it somebody gorgeous?'

'I've never been able to tell anyone who he is because the situation isn't straight-forward.'

'I see! It's complicated, is it? Is he married? How *very* intriguing!'

Flora saved her from any further disclosures by suddenly running up and tweaking at her arm. 'Mum . . . I've got to do twids.'

'Caroline,' Roz said, 'sorry to break off. We'll have to go and look for the cloakroom. See you in a minute.'

As she walked with Flora to the house, she took very deep breaths. She knew there was a lavatory in Daphne's house beside the garden door. While Flora was in there, she moved about the hall breathing slowly and sitting down on the telephone chair to stop herself feeling faint.

'The last person didn't pull the plug,' she said, coming out.

'Well, you do it. Then just wait a minute before you do twids. Mind your lovely dress.'

When Flora reappeared, she got up and glanced into the

dining room, guessing that the wedding presents might be on display somewhere.

'Flora, look, come and see Aunty Daphne's wedding presents.'

They were laid out on the refectory table, on the sideboard, on a serving table and a chest of drawers, as well as on the floor. Dinner services, silver, bed linen. Magnificent things as she'd known they were bound to be.

'They've got bicycles,' Flora said enviously. 'When can I have a bike?'

'Soon,' she replied vaguely, wondering how she was ever going to afford that.

'*Gone to London to become a whore.*'

If she stood still for a few minutes on her own, she might be able to calm herself. From across the lawn, the voices rose and fell, punctuated by loud laughs and happy little shrieks. She could see Tim sitting in a swing seat by the summer house. There was a band playing softly in the background. 'This is my lovely day. The day I will remember, the day I'm dying.'

'Oh Roz! There you are!' Daphne poked her head round the door. 'I've been looking for you. Do come up, while I get changed, will you? Flora, what a good girl you've been today. You made me a marvellous bridesmaid.'

Flora gave her a generous smile. 'When I'm getting married, I'll let you be my bridesmaid.'

'Well, don't leave it too long like your mother!'

Roz said, 'Daphne, what lovely things you and Glyn have been given.'

Daphne came and stood beside her. 'I haven't thanked you for your beautiful present. We were so touched because I know how difficult things must have been for you recently.

Mummy says Waterford glass must have cost you the earth. Glyn and I will certainly treasure it. Where's your sweet little card to us . . . yes, look, here it is.'

'*Daphne and Glyn*', the card read, '*With my love and very good wishes for much happiness* – Roz x x x'

It was nestling inside Professor Tunnicliffe's second best salad bowl.

TWELVE

'We 'ear all this twaddle these days about two men getting up to "anky panky together,' said Mrs, Hitchen, musing, as she rolled out her pastry for a steak and kidney pie, on a case of clerical indecency reported in last Sunday's *News of The World*, 'but, I mean to say, 'ow do they think two men are going to have sec? I can't see it.'

Sister Theresa, a nun, who was going to teach cookery at her convent, said nothing. And neither did Roz who was bored stiff.

'I think it's a load of nonsense meself, Vi,' her friend Mrs Lawler declared firmly, letting the crumbling flour fall lightly through her fat fingers, 'I've never heard anything about it before.'

'Well, I expect they probly just put their arms round each other, that's what it is,' Mrs Hitchen observed finally. 'And what's wrong in that?' She pursed her mouth and shook her head, a source of sexual knowledge to be reckoned with, beneath her small round purple hat.

'They go up the bum,' muttered a young man called Howard, who wanted to be a chef. Roz heard him but nobody else did.

'Try not to talk too much while you're working,' the

supervisor warned. 'Now, are we all ready to put our lovely pies in the oven?'

The only thing to be said about Thursdays, Roz thought to herself, was that they seemed to put Professor Tunnicliffe into a good humour. Whatever she made in her class that day at the Tech, she took home with her to Delmartin Road and he ate it for supper. To date, he'd been most enthusiastic. He enjoyed musing with her upon the ingredients and airing his opinion on how this or that particular dish was to be found wanting. In fact, the cookery classes had definitely stayed her departure from his employ. It had been touch and go for a week or two after the college dinner. He was furious with her.

Roz was genuinely shocked that he'd taken her party behaviour so much to heart, because to her the evening was an agreeable blur. She could remember the people she'd met but she couldn't remember what had happened. She tried hard to put her point of view to Professor Tunnicliffe, which was that if one went on a social outing, one surely had the right to expect one would not be treated like a servant, even if one was one.

'What is wrong, Rosemary, about our arrangement is that it is your job as my housekeeper to handle me, instead of which I seem to spend all my time thinking how to handle you. Like it or not, you are my servant. I don't particularly want to use such a word in your case but that is the fact. As such I don't begrudge the phenomenal number of drinks recorded in my name at that dinner although I consider you drank far too much. And it is not really up to you, as a girl half her age — my housekeeper to boot — to sail round the Senior Common Room like Lady Bountiful drawing out Lady

Jerningham about her past, holding the Fellows' hands and that sort of thing.

'But you didn't come near me. I had to talk to people.'

'Let us get this straight. I came to you again and again to try to introduce you to various people. I don't expect you to have a look at them and then refuse to meet them. It is not for you to be making choices from among my colleagues' guests as to whom you wish to speak to at any given time.'

'No, no, I know. I loved that evening and I'm sorry to have made you cross. I'm only saying that two or three times when you'd got landed with someone you were bored with, you used me to dump them on and skip away.'

'*Skip away!*' he repeated incredulously. 'I don't understand you, I'm afraid.' His eyes began their warning gleam behind his thick glasses.

'No, well,' she said hastily, 'all I can say is I'm very sorry. I had a lovely time and I was terribly grateful to you for inviting me.'

'We'd better say no more about it,' he replied.

To her horror another squall blew up a few days later when the Professor was waiting for her to come in from hanging out the washing. He wanted to make some amendments to the shopping list before he left for work. Tired of waiting, he stepped out into his garden.

'Here is Mrs Strang!' Roz called to him as a big, amiable, grey-haired head, with undershot jaw, popped up over the hedge.

He stared at it blankly bobbing above the pyracantha as if it was an Aunt Sally target. He said nothing to either of them and went back inside.

'You didn't say a word to Mrs Strang,' she said when she went in herself.

'What word should I have said?'

'Well, you could have said "Good morning". She'll be hurt now.'

'My dear girl, Mrs Strang won't be hurt. She knows me.'

'If I may say so,' Roz said carefully, 'it would be different if Mrs Strang was a beauty queen.'

'Indeed it would,' he agreed with a dry little woof.

'Yes and she knows that. That's the point. You have to be kind to plain women.'

'Rosemary, you will persist in behaving towards me as if you've got some trump cards up your sleeve. As I see it, you hold no cards at all. It would be wiser in the circumstances, I should have thought, to keep quiet and allow me to get on with my life in the way I always have.'

She stood listening to him getting his car out of the garage.

'Push off, you unkind little man,' she said, 'and don't come back.'

If she shut up, he seemed to take advantage of her meekness and ride roughshod over her. If she had anything to say, there was trouble. She went straight upstairs and took one of his brown blankets out of the ottoman. She cut it up to make a bear costume for Flora who was in a school play.

One afternoon, in late October, Howard, the would-be chef in the cookery class, invited her to go for a drink as they left the building together. Since Flora was going straight from school to a party, she agreed. She had nothing else to do before she picked her up and put Professor Tunnicliffe's supper in the oven. She never had anything else to do because she didn't know anyone to do it with. She had got to know other mothers, and she was invited by them to their children's gatherings, but she hadn't found any friends yet of her own choosing. There was no opportunity.

Howard was a colourless introverted young man of about twenty-seven who had obviously done very little since leaving school but had now decided to try and establish a proper career. He approached the cookery instruction in a flat methodical way, as if he was the only person in the room.

'I don't know your name,' he said as they walked along the road together.

Roz was most irritated to hear it, since names had been used ad nauseam in the class. 'It's Zuleika,' she said.

'Mine is Howard.'

'Yes I know.'

After a small silence he said, 'Are you planning to cook professionally, Zuleika, when you leave college?'

'I already do cook professionally,' she told him, 'I'm a housekeeper.'

She'd never seen his face crease up into a smile before, but at this it did. 'You don't look like one.'

'I'm no good at it, that's why. But I've got no money and I've got a child. There's nothing else I can do.'

'I want to have children.'

She sensed he envied her the status of being a parent. Telling a child what to do would add to his authority. 'Think twice,' she warned him. 'I mean I adore Flora but I think I've done things the wrong way round. I'm stuck in a job I don't want. I have no money and nowhere to go so I can't get out of it. I'm quite likely to get the sack and I have no friends. I don't know a soul in Oxford.'

'You sound as if you've got an inferiority complex, Zuleika,' he said in his flat way. 'That could be your trouble. Shall we go in here?' He led the way into a pub called The Two Brothers.

It was already crowded. 'Let's sit down over there,' she suggested, moving towards a space for two on a leather seat in the corner, and wishing she hadn't come. She squeezed determinedly through the crush to the remaining places.

'Hull—O,' said a male voice as she passed.

At first she thought she was being picked up.

'Roz?'

She turned round. It was Tim Benstead.

'Tim!' she said, absolutely delighted, then she had to introduce Howard.

'What are you drinking, Zuleika?'

She stood beaming. 'Oh thank you . . . um . . . I . . .'

'Babycham?'

'Can I have cider, please?'

'Zuleika?' Tim echoed, '*Zuleika*? Did I hear right?'

She laughed, putting her hands up to her face. 'How embarrassing!'

'One of your patients, I presume? Or have you taken up conjuring now?'

'We go to the same cookery class every Thursday.' She lifted her plastic carrier to show him her container of beef bourguignon. 'Oh, Tim, it is lovely to see you. Howard's just told me I've got an inferiority complex.'

'Is that why he's calling you Zuleika to boost your flagging confidence? Would it help you if I did the same?'

'Listen, stop it,' she said giggling, 'Please don't go on about it now. I'll explain another time.'

'Ah great . . . we're going to have another time, are we? This is an unexpected pleasure. How long do I have to wait for that? I've been waiting for a reply to my letter for two years.'

When Howard returned with their drinks, he took off his raincoat and sat down beside her.

'Tim's a friend from home,' she explained. 'We both come from Cheshire. He's going to be a brain surgeon.'

'I got the idea from Zuleika.'

'You told me you didn't know anybody in Oxford,' Howard said.

Tim slipped so easily into Roz's life that she scarcely noticed it was happening. She did feel happier, although it undoubtedly increased her financial problems, which had been growing by the month anyway. She never had any of her salary left at the end of the week. She nearly always had to dip into the housekeeping money and make frantic adjustments to Professor Tunnicliffe's shopping lists. She skimped and juggled in the kitchen. She'd had to change her route in order not to pass the newsagents where she owed fifteen pounds.

By the time she had to sell her lovely little Morgan, she was reduced to buying petrol one gallon at a time, sometimes half. She couldn't afford the insurance, or the road tax, and once things started to go wrong with it, she couldn't ever hope to come up with the huge sums she had to pay for repairs. Her pile of bills was mounting all the time. One day, to her utter horror, a bailiff called at the house. She had to give him Professor Tunnicliffe's camera.

As Christmas loomed, like a hideous nightmare, Professor Tunnicliffe announced, to her great relief, that he would be staying with friends in Florence for a fortnight over that period. It meant that Tim could move into the house with herself and Flora and spend Christmas Day with them.

After his term ended, Tim went home to see his parents and on the day before Christmas Eve, he arrived back in Oxford. He took Flora out to choose a tree and then they all three spent the evening decorating it.

'This is really going to be my best Christmas ever,' Flora declared, draping more tinsel over Tim than on the tree. 'Shall we play the hiding game in the dark now?'

Roz said, 'Not now. It's time for bed. Maybe on Christmas Day. We'll have to see.'

'Oh yes, yes, mum *please* . . . we haven't played the hiding game for *ages*. I know where I'm going to hide. I bet you can't guess.'

'Just whisper to me,' Tim murmured. 'Tell me your best hiding place.'

'It's a secret!' she shouted, 'You have to come and find me. But I have to creep back here before you catch me.'

I will catch you both!' Tim roared in a deep, dreadful voice holding up his hands like claws.

'Hee, hee, hee!' Flora squealed, already in a state of delicious excitement.

Neither Tim nor Roz had much money — all hers had gone on a first bike for Flora — but they managed a turkey and she cooked it very well having just had one to do in the cookery class. Tim gave her a beautiful pair of long, brown boots she had seen in Elliston & Cavell and after much agonising she wrapped up a silver candlestick belonging to the Professor and presented that to him.

She'd discovered it by chance — one of a pair — wrapped in green baize at the back of a little cupboard. She took it out and wrapped it in Christmas paper then she tore the wrapping off again and put it back. When the boots came, she had a sleepless night with the anxiety of everything, went back to the cupboard and retrieved it. If Professor Tunnicliffe suddenly had occasion to use his silver candlesticks, she would simply have to ask for it back. But she could meet that appalling eventuality if and when it happened.

Tim seemed staggered to receive silver from her. '*Roz*! But my darling girl, is my room at Trinity up to this?' He kissed her with melting tenderness in response to her grand gesture and their relationship jumped several notches within the next few hours. By that time though, she was sure he loved her and she sincerely hoped she loved him.

It was only an emotional event like the crowded midnight service at St Mary's The Virgin on Christmas Eve that brought on any doubts. At first, as the choir moved up the aisle to 'Once In Royal David's City', her very favourite carol, she was filled with a festive feeling of spiritual thankfulness to be standing so cosily beside Tim and Flora. This feeling expanded, as they sang their way lustily through the verses, to embrace thoughts of Ma, and past Christmases at home, until by the time they came to,

> '*And He leads His children on*
> *To the place where He is gone*'

she was completely overwhelmed by a piercing desolation. She felt her heart would break for Ivor.

But the quiet, empty, snowy Oxford days with Tim

were happy. They played murder with Flora, creeping stealthily all over the darkened house. The excitement reached its pitch when Tim took a white sheet from a bed and suddenly appeared like a ghost at the top of the stairs. Roz and Flora screamed in terror, and screamed and screamed, and tumbled hysterically to the bottom.

They went for walks balancing Flora, mute with concentration, on her new bicycle, and came back for tea, with hot buttered toast and jam, beside Professor Tunnicliffe's fire. His sitting room had taken on a comforting, day-after-the-bomb, most lived-in look from dust, squashed scattered cushions, old newspapers and shreds of Christmas paper strewn about the carpet which was speckled thickly with dropping needles from the tree.

Tim stayed on until the day before the professor was due back from Italy, then he went home again to his parents until term began. The house seemed quiet without him when he'd gone but Roz had a frantic time clearing up and no time for reflection.

The Professor arrived back in Delmartin Road in the middle of the day, and right into the middle of a skirmish with Mrs Strang over a lorry-load of manure, which was being backed into his gate instead of hers. He sprang from his car and ran down the drive on bent legs, calling out '*No, no, no!*' and making wild sweeping movements with his arm. Mrs Strang, horrified at the impending catastrophe and its consequences, hurried round to his gate in the nick of time.

All was well and communication at last established. The lorry did not dump the manure on the Professor's doorstep. He exchanged a few jocular words with Mrs Strang, and the driver, and came into the house, pleased with his powers for prompt action and the passing pleasantry. It was in this genial state that he greeted Roz and, because he was genial, so was she. The New Year started on a sunny note.

Sunniness shone over the routine in the house and Roz was feeling reasonably contented. Trapped, certainly, but not unhappy. She was looking forward to seeing Tim again and, if Flora was all right, which she was, that lifted her own spirits to the highest degree. She wasn't thinking about Ivor. He was, of course, always at the back of her mind, tucked eternally into his own compartment, with the satisfying footnote that his relationship with Caroline had come to an end.

Caroline's picture of them closeted together in seedy intimacy on tour, had made her realise what an 'also-ran' she actually was in Ivor's life — even if his mother had done her down. It was no longer realistic to imagine him dreaming of her as she'd done of him. But at least the way was clear for her to get in touch, establish his fatherhood of Flora and, apart from anything else, ask him to help with financial support. The rest was fantasy. Having Tim around had somehow given her the strength to face the situation in a more practical light. Even if her legs didn't buckle at the sight of Tim, she didn't want to lose him.

The day before he was due back in Oxford, she was in the Professor's study, leafing through his books while she was dusting and tidying, when she picked up a copy of the *Radio Times*.

She turned the pages over slowly just in case there was a good programme she might miss.

'JUST MARRIED!' was the headline above a short piece about a soprano — Eve Anthony — one of the BBC Singers. The picture showed lustrous, thyroidal eyes, (like Caroline's), a pert turned-up nose and thick sensual lips. Some sixth sense warned her even before she got to the thunderbolt. '... who has recently returned from her honeymoon in Ibiza, after marrying another singer, Manchester-born tenor ...' No, no, please let it not be ...

But it was.

Ivor married. Ivor fucking *married*. Oh ... God. The end. Shocked into a state of irrational depression, she greeted Tim.

Entertaining him when Professor Tunnicliffe was at home was a totally different matter from when the house was theirs. When the front door bell rang, Flora thundered down the stairs in her pyjamas with loud shrieks. His arrival created the maximum disturbance, it seemed to Roz, who watched nervously while he swung Flora up into the air. 'Whee ... hee ... heee!' he shouted. 'How's my best girl Flora? Have you missed me?'

'Shhh ...' Roz said, putting on a pained face and placing her finger to her lips. 'Professor Tunnicliffe is here!' she added in a loud bright voice, gesturing towards the dining room. 'We must keep very quiet because he doesn't like a lot of noise in his house. Come and sit in the kitchen.'

When she took his supper in to the dining room, the Professor was sitting stiffly at the head of his table, drumming his blunt manicured nails quietly. She made a point of earnestly explaining that she would be paying for Tim's share of their chicken curry out of her own money.

He gave a dismissive little wave with the back of his hand. 'Oh yes, yes ... thank you, Rosemary. That's all right. However, it may be more of a problem than you imagine having your friends here while you're looking after me. It may not be such a good idea, you know. You have your own time off. Away games only might suit us both better in future.'

She went into the kitchen and closed the door. 'I don't care how much I do that little man down,' she said grimly. 'Away games only — what an absurd arsehole he is.'

'The "arsehole" is quite an important philosopher, you know. Am I going to meet him?'

'No. He can't treat people properly. And you have no idea what it's like being put into this position and having to creep about like a numbskull and speak when you're spoken to. There's no money. Your opinion is of no account and, if it is offered, he pretends not to hear. If he says good morning, it's an act of graciousness. Sometimes he doesn't say it at all and that puts me in such a rage I can't speak to him. I am not allowed to be a person because I am a housekeeper, that's what it amounts to. When anybody comes — well, they hardly ever do because he's such an oddity — but one man did, and he said he thought most people had dreams about meeting the Queen. He was saying it to me as well and I was just answering, saying I didn't believe it was true and telling him what I did think people dreamt about, when tyrant Tunnicliffe said coldly "Yes, thank you, Rosemary." Well, if somebody is a humble housekeeper, you've got to . . .'

Tim laughed. 'There's nothing humble about you, baby doll.'

'Yes, it is laughable, but I'm not laughing, Tim. He'd like me to wear a uniform, you know, like a maid, to show up his status. I can only tell you that if my mother had met that woollen-headed little despot socially, she would scarcely have given him the time of day. Of course she was always polite and anxious to say she could mix with dukes and dustmen but, what I mean is, when I was running my own business, I didn't treat anyone like dog dirt.'

'From what I hear, it might have been better if you had.'

'Oh God, I'm so sick of it,' she said hopelessly, going to the stove to get their food. 'If it wasn't for Flora and her school and all her friends . . . Thank you for bringing that whisky. Can you give me some? Give me a lot. D'you think he's heard me ranting about him . . . oh hell, what do I care? I honestly don't know how I can survive anyway.'

'Come on, you're not going to be here for ever,' Tim answered soothingly.

The implication was, she knew, that she would be with him. And that assumption of his, coming on top of Ivor Mostance's marriage and Professor Tunnicliffe's high-handedness, only increased her agitation. If she hadn't been feeling so het up, she would have realised it would be a great mistake to tell Tim about Ivor, that night, when she was going to have to send him away so early. But she was totally unprepared for his reaction and, after all the whisky, she couldn't stop herself anyway. It laid the foundations for many rows to come. Tim was devastated when he finally learned who Flora's father was.

He could not let the matter drop. Each time they met he found a way of re-introducing it, reacting as furiously to everything she said as if Ivor had an existing role in their daily lives. What made matters worse was that she did not dare allow him to stay in her room, with Professor Tunnicliffe around, in case she lost her job. And that only served to increase Tim's very bad mood.

Apart from her time off, they met each day at the Cadena Café while she was shopping, and sometimes they walked afterwards in Christchurch Meadow. The first time they met at the Cadena, they were there from ten o'clock until it closed at six and she had to ring another mother to fetch Flora from school. The difficulty was, with Flora to look after, plus her duties, she had no other time to see him.

'I'm missing you,' he said morosely, biting into an éclair. 'When does Tunnicliffe go abroad to that conference?'

'In about a fortnight. Flora keeps asking when you'll be coming.'

Mention of Flora set him off again. 'To think of you producing her with that great posing, self-absorbed creep . . . Christ! I wish you'd never told me.'

How she wished it too. 'I only told you because I thought it was time I straightened the situation out.'

'But why d'you decide to straighten it out as soon as I come on the scene?'

'Tim, that's the whole point,' she explained earnestly, trying to be soothing. 'Having you beside me somehow makes it easier to tackle.'

'Why tackle it at all? You don't need him.' He pushed his hand into his hair and leant back, eyes closed, as if trying to unravel her thinking process. 'He's never bothered about you and Flora.' The eyes opened again, very blue and flinty, challenging.

'Mm . . . I know.' She sighed. 'Please don't go on and on at me. I can't stand it.'

'*You* can't stand it. Good God. What am I meant to feel about having that ballroom dancing show off hanging about here in his cloak and hat and poisoning our relationship?'

'Listen to me. A: he's just got married. Got that? B: it's

not his fault because he never knew he had a child. I've told you how his mother opened my letter to him and said she'd set a solicitor on to me. When it was happening I was too young and innocent and scared stiff and I was reeling from Ma's death as well. I've only recently discovered that she went round saying nobody knew whose baby it was, because I'd been out with so many people.'

'And had you? You certainly had no time for me I seem to recall.'

'Yes, but I thought I was involved with Ivor.'

'All right . . . so when it was clear he'd scarpered, why didn't you hire a lawyer to sort it out then?'

'Oh, Tim, for goodness sake, the last thing I could bear the thought of was some horrific legal imbroglio. I believed he loved me and I didn't need any money from him. By the way, that reminds me . . . I'm awfully sorry to say it, but can you lend me three pounds? I'm not going to have enough for the shopping now because I had to get shoes for Flora.'

Obediently, he reached into his wallet and handed her the notes.

'Thanks. You see, what I was saying was that I had to have something to hold on to. I was incapable of thinking "well that's over". I just sat moping in that place in Littlehampton, playing my records and hoping we'd come together sooner rather than later.'

'Meanwhile, he was scouring the country for you, no doubt, mounting anybody who crossed his path and singing his heartless heart out about moons and stars and true love being over the rainbow?'

She couldn't resist saying, 'Ivor was touring in a musical called *Zuleika*.'

'Oh no. Jesus! So now I see where Zuleika comes in. And I expect our smiling heart throb was playing the Duke of Dorset, was he?'

She was laughing. 'Shut up, stop it! Why can't you be a bit more aloof about everything? That's what women like.'

'Aloof?' His beaky face distorted. '*Aloof!* I'll leave you alone, you silly bitch, so you can behave like a mooning shop girl as you did with him. If Ivor Mostance was aloof, it was obviously because he didn't love you. He doesn't deserve to know he has a daughter like Flora.'

'Tim, I want her to know who her father is.'

'I forbid it!'

THIRTEEN

While the Professor was out of the country for ten days at a conference, Tim moved into the house again.

Roz's revelations about Ivor Mostance definitely had damaged the relationship. He hated the idea of Ivor having a stake in their future. The thought of Mostance lording it over him, and interfering in the upbringing of Flora, was anathema to him. He couldn't stand him. So he was suspicious and possessive, as if he anticipated trouble. He kept interrogating Roz, taunting her, almost as if he hoped to find her reactions wanting, as if he expected to be rewarded with one final good reason for not loving her. But he did love her. He couldn't help himself. She always made him think of a beautiful wild pony who would come trotting up to anyone to make friends, wait until the halter was produced to catch her, then gallop away like the wind. He'd imagined he was going to be the only one who could break her in to real life. His confidence had taken a significant dent on that score. They had started having a lot of rows because their circumstances were so difficult and, in any case, they both enjoyed fights. But, as long as they made up immediately afterwards, the making up was sublime.

Certainly, while he was sleeping at Delmartin Road, things were considerably more harmonious, because Tim felt more in control. Flora was a calming influence too. She adored Tim and neither of them would have wanted to start a scene in front of her.

A day or two before Valentine's Day, Roz stopped to buy a card for Tim on the way home from Flora's school.

'D'you think he'll like that? Don't tell him you've seen it, will you. It's a secret.'

'*To my darling Valentine*' was written on an envelope with a red heart in place of a stamp. Beneath it lay a single red rose.

Flora was definitely impressed. 'Is he my valentine too?' she asked anxiously.

'Yes he is.'

Flora looked pleased and thereafter rather preoccupied.

The next day she was quieter than usual when she came out of school. She went off to bed and appeared to have gone to sleep when Roz looked in. But when she got up in the night, she automatically glanced in again and, to her astonishment, Flora's bed was empty.

'Flora?'

There was no sign of her and no reply. At first she called her in a loud whisper so as not to wake Tim. When she'd looked into Professor Tunnicliffe's room and the child wasn't there, she began to grow worried. Where was she? She couldn't have gone downstairs, could she? Out of the house? Alarmed, she ran downstairs. Flora was curled up in a little naked heap on the front door mat.

'Flora! What on earth are you doing?'

Flora smiled sleepily. 'It's a secret.'

'But you've got nothing on. You're stone cold. Did you have a bad dream?'

'The post hasn't come,' Flora said.

'But it doesn't come till eight o'clock.'

'What time is it now?'

'It's three o'clock. The middle of the night. Come to bed.'

'But I've got to wait and see if my valentine comes.'

'Who from?'

'It's from me and it's a secret. To my darling Valentine. Don't tell Tim.'

When Professor Tunnicliffe returned from his conference in Canada, she was reluctant to banish Tim from the house again. With her heart in her mouth, she smuggled him up to her bedroom each evening while the Professor was having dinner. As he seemed to be none the wiser, the arrangement turned into a habit.

Tim read or watched television until she joined him. He kept a bottle of whisky hidden in the room and tried to stop Roz drinking too much of it. A lot of scotch made her get very angry.

'No, I'm not letting you have any more,' he said, one night, as she held out her glass again. They were lying on her bed whispering together. He reached down to get the bottle off the floor and held it up. 'Jesus! Look how much you've drunk. You'll be like a zombie in the morning.'

'Ooh . . . how much *you've* drunk, you mean. You taught me to drink. It never comes into my head when you're not here.'

'You make up for it when I am. Anyway, it's bad for you and it makes you turn nasty.'

'Rubbish. It makes me all the more dulcet. It's just that women naturally speak out. Men are so cryptic.'

'Roz, it's one o'clock and I'm dog tired. I have an essay to read out in the morning. I want to be able to focus on it.'

'Come on, we'll have one more. I'm too tired to go to bed. I do marvel at you being able to write these essays. I shouldn't be able to concentrate now. Well, of course, I don't suppose I ever did.'

'You should do a degree.'

'No woman from our existence has gone to a university.'

'No woman from our existence has become a housekeeper.'

She glowered at him and started to bite her nails. 'How could I start studying with Flora to cope with and all this housekeeping and cookery? Anyway, I haven't got the right exams even to embark on a degree. Do you realise that not a single person from Firth House has done a degree? It wasn't mentioned. The emphasis was on good manners and having a straight back. In any case, I thought I was going to be with you.'

'I won't be able to support you for ages in the manner to which you wish to become accustomed again.'

'No, I know that, but you do want me with you?'

'Of course.'

'Well, why are you urging me to get off somewhere else and do a degree?'

'I'm only pointing out to you that times are changing. If you're going to have to work, you might as well get some qualifications and try to do a job you enjoy. I know it's difficult while Flora's young but, when she's older, you'll need something to do.' He patted her thigh in a hearty avuncular manner. 'You can't be a party girl all your life.'

'A party girl? I beg your pardon?'

'Keep your voice down or old Tunnicliffe will hear you.'

'A *party girl*,' she repeated incredulously. '*What*? I ran my own business in London, you big dolt, while you were probably still in the school playground.'

'And that got you where you are today,'

'How can I help it if I was robbed by my partner? He's done everybody down. He's in jail now for not paying his wives anything, and I'm not getting a penny out of him.'

'Well, it all sounds pretty rackety to me. You had no sensible relationships.'

'Are you mad? Hordes of men asked me to marry them.'

He yawned at her, with his mouth wide open like a lion, in what she took to be a deliberately disrespectful manner because she hadn't got a degree. 'Oh, I'm not talking about those aimless deadbeats you entertained from your boudoir in Shepherd Market.'

'Richard Kitchener, you stupid swine, was hardly an aimless deadbeat. Richard Kitchener was one of the finest men I've ever met. Men like him don't grow on trees, I can assure you. I could have been the district officer's wife in Fiji if I'd wanted to be.'

'So you never fail to point out. Didn't you throw your shoes at him at a dinner party and put him off the idea?'

'That man loved me to the last. Unlike you. Look here, I'm sick to death of you giving me these insults. Just shut up and leave me alone if you're so contemptuous. Perhaps you'd better just go home.'

'I'll go in the morning. I knew you'd start behaving badly if you had another drink.'

'You'd better go right away because you're making me livid. Why be so hurtful all the time?' She heaved him towards the edge of the bed. 'Why come here all the time if you think I'm just a party girl. At least I'm better looking than those swots I see all over the place.'

'Yes, I like party girls.'

'Yes, well, I don't like you so don't ever come back, please.'

'If I go, silly bitch, I'm not coming back.' He emphasised his words with his teeth bared, gnashing them together in a ridiculous manner, like a dog eating a spider. 'And I'm the last sensible offer you're likely to get because you're mad. D'you know that? You live in a bloody dream world. God help any man who loves you! When he left you, Mostance made the only wise move he's probably ever made in his life.'

She tipped the rest of her drink over his head. 'Bugger off! You vile bugger!'

'Right!' He seized the sheet and dramatically smothered his dripping face in it. 'Right! You've asked for it and now you're going to get it!' He leapt off the bed and with wild, furious movements he began to collect his discarded clothes off the floor.

When he'd gathered them into a bundle, he opened the bedroom door and, still naked, went into the bathroom.

Roz lay listening, trying to tell what he was doing. Now he'd gone, she wanted him to come back. She supposed he must be washing the whisky out of his hair but, when he didn't reappear, she got up to go and bring him back to bed.

To her horror, as she was about to step out onto the landing, Professor Tunnicliffe's door opened suddenly. He emerged in his navy nightshirt and padded to the bathroom. He tried the door, found it locked, and went back into his room.

There was silence.

About ten minutes passed in which Roz put on her nightdress and combed her hair. She was concerned to see that she was very red in the face.

Professor Tunnicliffe's door opened again and he hurried across the landing to try the door again. Finding it still locked, he coughed and muttered to himself as he withdrew.

She didn't know what to do. If she attempted to whisper to Tim that it was safe to come out, the chances were they'd bump into each other and he'd find out that she'd defied him and arranged a home game.

She stayed where she was, behind the door, pins and needles in her leg, hoping he'd dropped off.

He hadn't.

For his third attempt to gain entry to his own bathroom half an hour later, he'd donned his dressing gown, slippers and his spectacles. He rattled the door handle and called out, 'Rosemary? Is that you? Is anything the matter?'

She felt sure he would hear her heart thumping.

'Is it Flora?'

Suddenly she heard him coming towards her room. He tapped on the door and she made a flurry of movement to indicate she was getting out of bed.

'Ah, Rosemary,' he said, looking irritated. 'Is there somebody in the bathroom?'

'Um . . .'

'Look, I thought we'd agreed away games only. That must be your friend from Trinity in there, is it?'

She gave her head a small, sleepy shake. 'I don't think so?'

'Well, surely you must know who it is,' he answered, getting his gleaming, glassy look, 'or else it means we must have an intruder in the house and I'd better call the police.'

She strode to the bathroom door and tried the handle. 'Is she still here?' she asked, in a loud, hectoring tone.

'Is it Flora?'

'No, no, I think Flora's asleep.' She went to the child's bedroom and looked round the door. 'No, no, she's fast asleep. It must be Elspeth Nightingale,' she added, mentioning the one name that might be acceptable to the Professor. 'My cookery teacher.'

'Why should she barricade herself in my bathroom in the middle of the night?'

'Yes,' Roz agreed, wrinkling her brow.

'Could you ask her to come out?'

'Elspeth?' She knocked on the door several times. 'Are you all right? Could you come out, please.'

Silence.

'I think we'd better leave her, Professor Tunnicliffe. I'm so sorry. But I think she may have fallen asleep on top of her busy day.'

'Really, Rosemary, I should have thought that was most unlikely. Is she staying the night? Why is she here?'

'She kindly called after you'd gone to bed to drop in some new recipes for you. We had a chat and I thought she'd gone home. She must have slipped into the bathroom instead. Quite honestly, I think it's better to leave her. I'm sure she'll come out as soon as she can.'

The Professor gave her a look of total disbelief.

'Miss Nightingale?' He hammered on the door. 'This is Hugh Tunnicliffe. Can you hear me? Can you take the key out of the lock and push it under the door then we can let you out.'

A further half hour went by.

'I think we have to reach the dreadful conclusion that she's taken ill,' sighed Professor Tunnicliffe.

'Ye . . as,' Roz agreed, in quite a sanguine way. 'It may be over-eating.'

'Let's hope she hasn't had a stroke, or something. She's obviously unconscious. I think we'll have to force the door. Better that than being charged with manslaughter,' he added, with an appalled little woof.

'Dear me,' Roz said, using an expression she'd got from him. 'That seems rather drastic.' She pinched her mouth hard then suddenly whipped herself out of sight and stood hooped behind her door until she'd controlled herself.

With bent knees and a Quasimodic vigour, the Professor was jerking out the ottoman, on its stiff old wheels, into the middle of the landing.

'Now, Rosemary,' he commanded breathlessly, 'I shall need your help.'

At the thought of Tim behind the door, she let out some fearful jackdaw yaps of laughter. 'I do hope it doesn't cause my womb to drop!'

He manoevered the ottoman into position directly opposite the bathroom door.

'Professor . . . no don't! Listen, please don't damage

the door. Let's pick the lock. Wait a minute ... it's not necessary ... just let me ...' She tried to clutch his arm.

He had never known such aggravation. He was quite beside himself with rage. Was a man entitled to get into his own bathroom, or was he not? Grunting with exertion, he heaved the ottoman on its way. It crashed into the bathroom door. The thin wood juddered and splintered, the lock broke and the door swung open.

The bathroom was empty.

The two of them stood there together united in their speechless amazement.

'My mustard towel seems very wet,' Professor Tunnicliffe remarked, in a defeated, wondering voice. 'And there is no key to be seen.'

'Perhaps Elspeth absent-mindedly locked the door on the outside as she left the house,' Roz murmured, sobering up into a state of shocked relief. 'She's so used to locking up.'

'It was an intruder,' he said, pushing open the unlatched window. If his original suspicion crossed his mind, he didn't mention it. After a lifetime with students, he knew when he was beaten.

'What's happening?' Flora demanded, coming to her door. 'Why are you awake?'

At the same moment, sleepless Mrs Strang got out of bed next door to make herself a cup of tea. As she peered out of her window she saw a figure silhouetted high up against the side of Professor Tunnicliffe's house. He was clinging precariously to a drainpipe. She called the police.

Tim saw the lights from the police car turning into

Delmartin Road. He slid down, tearing his clothes and spraining an ankle as he dropped. He escaped over the hedges and disappeared into the darkness.

FOURTEEN

Nothing more was said about the bathroom door debacle. Her communication with Professor Tunnicliffe was affected by it, however. Although there had never been a rich flow of robust discourse between them, it now rarely rose above a stilted trickle. She tried her best to make amends but the poor man had an undisguisedly beleaguered look about him. Whenever they did have a nervous conversation together, she fancied she saw the whites of his eyes.

Towards the end of the Trinity Term he announced that he would like to have a dinner party at Delmartin Road. It struck a chill within her but she was determined to show that she meant well and to make it up to him by making sure it was a memorable occasion.

'One of my old friends from Austria, Herwig Kogonickel will be coming, with a Mrs Krystal Bradley and Lord Sturton. I think you can manage dinner for four, can't you? We must get things right this time. I think we'd better discuss the menu in some detail beforehand. We might even have a practise run. What d'you think?'

Tim called the afternoon she was cleaning all the silver. Spoons and forks were heaped on newspaper on the kitchen table with pieces from the best dinner service which still had to be washed.

'You're very busy today. What's all this then?'

'Prof Tunnicliffe is having a dinner party.'

'Am I invited?'

She laughed as she filled the kettle. 'Good God, no. Your name is mud in this house. Well, actually its Elspeth Nightingale.

'I thought you said he was getting over it.'

'Yes, but it's not the same. We never had wondrous communication but he no longer corrects my grammar, and that sort of thing, which is a sad sign of lost intimacy, isn't it. I'd be saying 'Flora and I' and he'd say 'Flora and me.' It was rather sweet.'

He nodded, getting the point. 'I was hoping you'd come for a walk?'

'I can't. But we could have tea and then go down and collect Flora, couldn't we. D'you know at her age, I was riding my bicycle to school. Now, I wouldn't dream of letting her come home alone.'

'I can always do it for you.'

'She'd love that.'

Tim's exams had finished, so he was at a loose end. He'd invited her to the Trinity Ball but she'd told him she couldn't go because she hadn't got a dress. She found it difficult enough to cope within the limits of her own restricted little life, without stepping outside that to meet even bigger demands. They were meant to be having two weeks in Scotland in August, with Flora, but she had no idea how she was going to raise her share of the money for that. A part of her wished Tim would fail his exams. She could feel him sliding out of her reach already, and with her blessing. She no longer felt she had the stamina to keep up.

She had sleepless nights over her overdraft. She had managed to bamboozle Mr Nelson of Lloyds Bank with her talk of a twenty thousand pound investment in a London business. She couldn't tell him the truth. Even when Basil came out of prison, he'd go on doing her down. Susceptible to her smiles, because she pulled out all the stops at their interviews, the manager pulled himself together between visits and wrote cold, frightening letters enquiring when the bank might expect to see any of these monies and threatening to stop her cheques — which he did from time to time — when she left his letters unopened. She walked into the bank each week to draw money, with her legs literally buckling. But for the housekeeping, she could never have managed on her salary. When she was cutting the mould off the professor's loaf because she had no money to buy a fresh one, she knew this must be rock bottom. She'd never dared to tell Tim how bad a mess she was really in. She didn't want to appear too pitiful for words.

Tim picked up a salt cellar, breathed on it and started to polish it till it gleamed. 'There you are. Look at that.'

'You're a great help to me,' she said smiling. 'I've got to bring more stuff out of the cupboard in his study. Can you come up there with me?'

'I've got nothing else to do.'

'Your life is one of continual self-sacrifice.'

'You're wrong there,' he replied, putting his hand up her skirt as they went up the stairs. 'The price for this is going to be very high.'

While she lifted things out of the cupboard to get at some side plates and a gravy boat, he looked at the books which lined the walls and lay piled on every surface round the room.

'Tunnicliffe's an impressive chap, isn't he?'

'I suppose he is. I mean, you have to have nerves of steel to be a don, don't you, really. They're very gracious and civilised on top but, by Jove, they are fighty underneath.'

'Who's coming to dinner?'

'The dinner's for some visiting Austrian classics academic — Herwig Pumpernickel.'

'Pumpernickel?'

'Perhaps not . . . something like that anyway. Also a Mrs Bradley, psychologist, who remembers him from the past and Lord Sturton who composes music. I've met him. He rides a bicycle wearing a wool hat in winter and pale blue shorts in summer. He's most charming and very fond of food. He brings Flora jelly babies.'

'Your man Pumpernickel . . . classics, did you say? Well, hey look at this! I've found the very thing you need for your dinner.'

'What is it?' She went on stacking china.

'A Roman cookery book — it's got recipes for stuffed doormice and Pullus Parthicus — that's chicken in the Parthian Way. You could do a special menu for them.'

'What a narrow escape I've had. I'm surprised he hasn't drawn it to my attention. Now come on, I've got to get moving. She glanced at the little book then pointed to the cupboard. 'I'm taking these dishes down. Can you bring those plates for me and the gravy boat.'

As he turned to do it, her heart stood still. Too late, she saw the lone silver candlestick protruding from its green baize cover. For a second she hesitated but she could do nothing except to walk out of the room praying he was not going to notice it.

He didn't follow her immediately. There was silence.
She waited.
'Tim!'
No answer.
'T . . i . . m!'
'Yes.'
'Aren't you coming down?'

He came very slowly down the stairs. She didn't even have to look at him to know he was holding the candlestick which matched the one she'd given him as a Christmas present. She busied herself at the kitchen table.

Tim held the candlestick in his right hand and tapped it against his left palm.

She looked up. 'Oh Lord,' she said, stumbling over the words. 'You shouldn't have got hold of that! I was going to give you that one for your birthday.'

'Wouldn't Professor Tunnicliffe miss it?'

The situation might have been saved if she'd said 'He hasn't missed the other one'. But he looked so stern, so dead honest and so brain surgeonish.

'No, no, Tim . . . it's mine.' She couldn't help gabbling. 'I've got things of my own in that cupboard. Things from home as well.'

'I think I'd better bring my candlestick back in time for the dinner party.' His voice had an unnatural, cool, thin lightness about it which she had never heard before.

With the Roman cook book in front of her, Roz was stuffing a hare by the time the Professor arrived home. She had most of the ingredients: almonds, pepper, oregano, chopped nuts, chopped hare giblets, chicken liver, and three eggs for binding. She'd left out pine kernels because they were expensive and she didn't know what *liquamen* was. The rich sauce was to be made from dates, pepper, onion, unspiced wine in this instance, and cornflour for thickening. A lot of stuff, but still cheaper than roast beef. She'd switched to the Roman recipe upon the devasting discovery that she hadn't enough money to provide that.

She had been humming quietly to herself with the utter relief of being able to replace the beef with such an inspired substitute for Professor Tunnicliffe's stately guests. When she heard his key turn in the lock she felt a wave of sickening apprehension. Would he be pleased that she was cooking an authentic Roman meal? As the Roman Empire grew, she'd read in the book, classical Greek cookery became the standard food of the middle and upper-classes. He was so steeped in all this stuff from Ancient Greece. Surely he would be touched that she'd attempted such a festive tribute to the Austrian classics academic? She put on her dark glasses to greet him.

She heard him go into the dining room where the table was already laid. It looked lovely. The silver was positively gleaming and pretty scarlet napkins matched a dainty floral arrangement in the middle of the table. She listened to him striding about the room, muttering to himself, pulling up the blinds and opening a window. She tiptoed to the kitchen door to guage his reaction to her efforts but all she caught was 'Fuck it! Fuck it!'

She hastened to the door of the dining room. 'What are you saying fuck for?' she demanded, dismayed.

He wheeled round. 'I beg your pardon?'

'What's wrong? Why are you saying "fuck it!"?'

His face was quite menacingly blank. 'I'm afraid I don't understand you.'

'You were saying "fuck it! fuck it!"'

'Stop!' He stepped backwards with an arm across his face as if to shield himself from further obscenity.

'*You* said it.'

'Rosemary, I would never dream of using such language. I was merely remarking that this room is fuggy. That is why I have opened the window.'

It was on this unhappy note of misunderstanding that the evening commenced.

'The beef is in the oven, I take it?'

'No, no . . not . . .'

'No? But my guests will be here at seven-thirty.'

'I know but you see, it's not beef. It's hare . . . an authentic Greek meal for the middle and upper-classes.'

'Greek? What are you talking about? Mr Kogonickel is an Austrian.'

'It's an ancient meal. Ancient Greece is his business. Look, just wait a minute.'

She brought him his cookery book. He stared at the recipes for hare, stuffed doormice, pig's stomach, black pudding and one for snails which had to be fattened in milk and salt with the excrement being removed from the mixture, when necessary. His mouth fell open as he read and he made a wheezing sound as if he was fighting for breath.

'Oh dear me,' he said, very weakly. His whole body seemed to sag.

To reassure him, Roz said, 'Yes, but I'm not doing anything *outré* tonight.'

'How could you have embarked on this major change

of plan without any consultation whatsoever? Rosemary, I have to say that I'm aghast.'

'It'll be all right. I promise you. I thought you'd be pleased.'

Professor Tunnicliffe studied the instructions for stuffed hare. 'Yes, yes, but date sauce . . .' he mused doubtfully, 'I don't know, Rosemary. I shouldn't make too much of that if I were you. Perhaps it will be all right. I sincerely hope so. I'd better leave you to it.' He turned, with a faint smile, as he left the kitchen. 'D'you know what Martial said? *Cum cenaret, erat tristior ille, domi.* When he dined at home he was the more depressed,' he translated with a little stifled woof.

The guests arrived promptly and Roz was all ready for them. She could hear their voices from the sitting room where they were drinking sherry. The Austrian's voice was deep and cavernous, Mrs Krystal Bradley's was a sort of staccato psychologist's yap, punctuated by laughs of near-hysteria and Lord Sturton, in his black, velvet jacket and tartan trews, had already popped into the kitchen to give her jellies for Flora.

'Ready when you are, Rosemary!' called Professor Tunnicliffe.

In the last few minutes of heat and haste, she opened the kitchen door to the garden. Mrs Strang's tabby, Tibby, streaked in with a present for her. Excited by the smell of hare, he dumped his own more humdrum mouthful while he sniffed his way among the waiting dishes. In search of more delights, he passed through into the sitting room.

The Austrian jumped to his feet, his arms waving. 'No, no, not cat! Cat must not come in, I am sorry to tell you. No cat ... no cat. I am most allergic to this animal.'

Roz raced into the room to collect him. 'I'll take him out. He lives next door.'

Mr Kogonickel subsided into his chair, relieved. 'I am glad to hear he does not live here ... ha ha! They are not friends of mine.'

Her first course, cold asparagus patina, was a great success. No sooner had she placed the dish of mashed asparagus tips, cooked in wine, onion and fresh coriander, onto the table than Lord Sturton bounded in and, in the aristocratic manner, helped himself first and started eating.

'Wonderful!' he told the others as they took their places.

'Herwig, my housekeeper had the idea of using authentic recipes from my Roman cookery book in your honour,' Professor Tunnicliffe explained. 'I believe she has used celestial seasonings which will prolong our lives.' He teased his guests with a playful little smile.

'Oh hoh, hoh, hoh, hoh,' laughed Mr Kogonickel.

'How intriguing,' responded Krystal Bradley, grey-haired and rosy, nodding her head very fast. 'I think this is terribly intriguing. What is this, dear?'

'This is sieved asparagus cooked in wine.' Roz smiled charmingly over her shoulder as she moved, poised and capable, and still wearing her dark glasses, towards the door. 'Nothing *outré* on the menu tonight! You won't be getting stuffed doormice!'

'What a sweet girl,' yapped Mrs Bradley, grateful to be dining with three attentive men.

Mr Kogonickel stared suspiciously at a tiny thread from a tea towel clinging to his plate. 'Is this hair of cat?'

From the kitchen as she dished up the vegetables, Roz listened to the conversation. The stuffed hare was sitting ready on the hot plate, its exotic filling bursting forth in mysterious succulent lumps.

Lord Sturton was telling them about a recent cruise round the Scottish Isles and how to hire a bicycle.

'Herwig and I had a rapturous holiday on the Danube thirty years ago,' Mrs Bradley confided to him. 'Since then I've had three nervous breakdowns. I've been in the Warneford recently having psychiatric treatment.'

Not at all disconcerted, Sturton took another helping from the asparagus dish. 'I expect they made you very comfortable, didn't they?'

'Oh very,' she agreed, nodding vigorously. 'You see I imagined that certain people were trying to poison me.'

Professor Tunnicliffe raised the serving spoon. 'A little more, Herwig?'

'No, no, thank you, Hugh. I am saving myself ... ha, ha, ha ... for what is coming!'

'Very good, Rosemary,' the Professor murmured, as she removed their plates, 'although we might have had candles tonight if we'd thought about it.'

She returned to the table carefully carrying the simmering hare and placed it before him. He reached out to stir the rich dark sauce, closing his eyes to bathe his senses in the ancient satisfying aroma. 'Well, well,' he said.

Roz helped to serve the vegetables then there was a little silence as they tasted the authentic meal.

'Yes,' said Lord Sturton, smacking his lips, 'definitely celestially seasoned!'

Krystal Bradley nodded. 'I agree with you ... this is *awfully* good.'

CELESTIAL SEASONINGS

Nobody was eating faster than Herwig Kogonickel. He scarcely had time to raise his hand in a humorous sign of victory. 'My compliments to the cook!'

The next moment, with a cavernous cry, he rocked backwards in his chair. His napkin flew to his mouth and he retched.

'Mouse!' he stuttered, pointing to his plate.

'No, no, Herwig,' Professor Tunnicliffe said. 'We're not eating doormice.'

'Mouse from cat!' his guest insisted dramatically. 'Excuse me.'

As Roz came hurrying into the room, he lurched past her.

'What's happened to Earwig Pumpernickel?'

'He's been poisoned, dear,' said Mrs Bradley. 'I expect they were trying to get me.'

Professor Tunnicliffe put a hand across his eyes. 'Mr Kogonickel has been taken ill, I'm afraid, Rosemary.' His expression was pained as he paused to listen to a terrible barking coming from the cloakroom.

'He seems to feel the food is tainted in some way by Mrs Strang's cat. Can this be true? Though rich, I'm bound to admit, the ingredients are quite pure,' he reassured Lord Sturton and Mrs Bradley. He peered over at the Austrian's plate. There, lying in the date sauce, dead but undefiled, was a small field mouse donated to the Roman dinner by Tibby.

FIFTEEN

After the night of the Roman dinner party, Professor Tunnicliffe made it clear that he'd had all he could take. He would like Roz and Flora out of his house at their earliest convenience. He wasn't unpleasant, although unnervingly for them, he had already started interviewing possible candidates while they were still there. He intended in future to employ a respectable, middle-aged widow with a lifetime's housekeeping experience behind her. He didn't seem to give much thought as to what was going to happen to Rosemary and her daughter. It had been an unfortunate experiment. He had allowed himself to be beguiled by her in the first place. Perhaps he'd thought he could mould her. But he knew trouble when he saw it and he'd seen it on their first meeting.

Roz remained polite to him, although she was embarrassed and humiliated when these capable, confident new women appeared for their interviews and, advised by Tim, she had to state most adamantly that she could not possibly move out of his house until there was somewhere else for her to go. Professor Tunnicliffe sighed and stared at his finger nails and told her she was making the situation extremely inconvenient for him. He did not want to start the next term with the matter left up in the air. They must set a definite date for her departure.

So, when that date arrived, and she had found no place to go to with Flora, she packed up all their things, (with several of his as well,) and went to stay with Daphne Phelps-Phillips, (now Daphne Jones), who was living in a big red-brick farmhouse in Leicestershire, surrounded by many framed wedding photographs and fat pigskin photo albums, full of oddly-assorted groups from that bizarre day. It increased her depression to look out of the windows only to see flat fields and not a soul, not a car, not a building in sight. Not many trees even. Flora was equally distressed by their sudden departure from Oxford.

She missed her friends, particularly her best friend, Sarah Meakin. 'But when am I going to see Sarah again?' she kept saying.

'As soon as we're settled,' Roz assured her wretchedly, wondering when that could possibly be. 'We'll invite her to come and stay with us. That'll be quite exciting, don't you think?'

'No,' said Flora. 'It won't be.'

The one person who was delighted with the temporary arrangement was Daphne. 'Please stay as long as you like, Roz,' she said, 'and I really do mean that. It's so nice to be having our lovely chats again.' Marriage to Glyn was beginning very gradually to pall.

The self-effacing little chap in the old, brown cap had taken on rather a swagger since he'd stopped being a farm labourer and become a landowner. He drove about in a Mercedes with his nose poking over the wheel and when he came in in the evening he liked to switch on the television for general knowledge quiz games. He lounged noisily, drinking from a can and eating crisps with his mouth open, and if he knew an answer he called it out in a boastful manner turning to Daphne with a triumphant smirk to show her that he knew more than she did. Roz found it most irritating, since she thought him a complete idiot who knew nothing about anything.

The trouble was, Daphne confided to her, Glyn was convinced that what he really knew about was making money and she had a great deal of that herself already. All his schemes involved worse conditions for the animals which upset her.

'We argue a lot,' she admitted, 'because Glyn's a businessman. I don't care if the farm just ticks over but he wants to expand. For instance, he wants to keep all our beautiful hens inside in battery sheds.'

'Good Lord,' Roz answered, horrified, 'you can't have a factory farm.'

'I know. I hadn't realised how hard it is to have a farm and be fond of animals,' Daphne sighed. 'Luckily, this area is good for crops and we've already won a prize for our milk. Anyway, I'm certainly not allowing Glyn to have pigs because I've seen what modern farming is like for the sows.

'It's funny, isn't it, I had this romantic vision of us pottering about together in our wellingtons but he doesn't want me out in the mud helping him. I think he's always hoping he'll come in and find me lounging about waiting for him in a black negligee or something. He's far more houseproud than I am. He wants pink walls and dainty drapes and no dogs sitting on chairs.' She sat, fondling the black labrador who was lying beside her on the sofa with his head on her knee as she spoke.

'An animal is an animal,' Glyn said, coming in at that moment. 'It's wrong to treat them like humans.'

Roz was glad she'd got an opportunity to put her spoke in. 'Yes, but surely animals respond and blossom with good treatment; I mean the more you humanise them, the more they respond, and they become depressed and frustrated with bad treatment.'

'Nobody's talking about *bad* treatment.' He gave her a knowing little smile. 'I expect Daphne's been complaining to you, has she, about my plans to modernise this place? I know she'd like me to float about in cloud cuckoo land with her, but man has always used animals for survival, Roz. We've got millions of mouths to feed in this world. That's why all the animals were put on earth.'

'Is it? We're told in the Bible to eat the green herb and take care of animals. They ought to be given a decent life and a decent death. If they're given unnatural conditions, and a restricted conveyor belt life, it's not a step forward, surely, in civilisation, it's a step back.'

'Let's face it,' Glyn said, turning a bit sullen and switching on the television, 'we don't know what God wants, do we? He may still want burnt offerings for all we know.'

'No, no, the Bible says he got sick of the stink of fat flesh.' She laughed inwardly that she remembered such a thing. 'In Isaiah, Glyn, now listen to this. God says, what is the purpose of your sacrifices? He says "I delight not in the blood of bullocks".'

But he wasn't listening. His Popeye-like head was already turned towards the screen. One day Daphne was going to say to him, 'Shut up, you foolish little man', and she hoped it was sooner rather than later before he'd laid hands on all her money and set up a monstrous empire of intensive farming.

'Don't have the poor hens crammed into battery cages with their beaks cut off,' she pleaded quietly to Daphne, and Daphne shook her head in acquiescence, whilst smiling with motherly indulgence at her husband who was going to tread on the head of whatever crossed his path now he had some power to do it.

The main advantage about farm life, as far as Roz was concerned, was that it kept Flora occupied. She helped with the milking, collected eggs and fed the cats and she had rides on Daphne's old, black Welsh mountain pony, Meg.

One morning, while Glyn was saddling Meg, he said to Roz, 'I can remember you out riding, careering along the verges bringing all the traffic to a standstill!'

'Yes, I remember you. We always waved, didn't we.'

'You ought to let Flora have a pony of her own.'

'I'd love her to have one, but we haven't got anywhere to live yet and when we do there won't be any money for that, I'm afraid.'

'If you get something round here, we'll have to see what we can do. There's plenty of good sound animals going dirt cheap. I could scout around for a good'un going for slaughter at the sales. You could keep it here and then we might see a bit more of you.'

Unlikely as it was, Roz thought he seemed to be giving her a look of bold intimate promise. She turned away and patted Meg.

'Daphne'd like that too.'

Flora gave an excited squeal. 'Oooh, yes, mum . . . please! Could we . . . *please?*'

'Well, thank you, Glyn, but actually we've arranged to

go and live as near as possible to Tim as soon as he gets his first hospital job.'

This was not true. Tim had offered to help. His parents had invited them to stay. But he had no job yet and she had no money. They couldn't slump onto his family like a ton of bricks. She was embarrassed enough about the candlestick episode anyway. She felt unfit for Tim. She knew he was going to make a fine brain surgeon and he'd push her into doing A levels and getting a degree. She couldn't, at this very moment, live up to him. Anyway, their telephone calls had to be too brief to achieve more than merely keeping in touch.

When he was out of sight, he tended to be conveniently out of mind as well. It was Ivor she thought about as she did the ironing. Ivor, she and Daphne talked about when they did the washing up. 'I'd like to marry Tim when I grow up,' was how she explained her feelings to Daphne. 'But I'd like to marry Ivor tomorrow', was what she admitted to herself.

Their departure from Daphne's house came suddenly, without warning, leaving precious little leeway for any choice of location.

Roz had thought no more about Glyn giving her the glad eye. She didn't know whether she'd imagined it. But when Flora went riding in the mornings she kept out of the way. Glyn was teaching her to ride bareback now, so when she'd helped him to feed the animals, he simply put a head collar on Meg, hoisted Flora up and left her to go round the field on her own. Sometimes Roz would hear him shouting 'Grip with your knees!' then she'd look out of the window to see old Meg trotting with the utmost reluctance and Flora bobbing about precariously in her red shorts on her ample back. If only Ivor had been able to see her growing up.

When she came in, she'd tell them how Meg was doing that day and proudly describe her own progress.

'Meg shied at a pile of leaves blowing about but I stayed on . . . Meg nearly scraped me off under the trees. When I call Meg she looks up then when she knows it's me she comes cantering straight at me and suddenly stops before she knocks me over. She blows down her nose then I give her some carrots.'

One morning she came racing into the house, calling out in great excitement. 'I've taught Meg to shake hands,' she said triumphantly. 'When I say "How d'you do," she holds up her hoof. Come and see. Please can you give me some more sugar lumps then I can show you.'

As Daphne was obediently opening the packet to get the sugar, Flora went up behind her and giggled. 'I don't think Uncle Glyn knows how to lift girls of my age up properly,' she remarked. 'When he was lifting me onto Meg this morning, his finger got stuck in my pants.'

For Roz, the scene suddenly transformed to slow motion. She saw Daphne's back go stiff. She stood stock still, her head up, her hands left in the air as if she no longer knew what she was doing or where she was. She didn't speak but then her hands fumbled with the packet. She put it back in the cupboard, shut the door then opened it and took the sugar out again.

'Flora, Uncle Glyn is too busy in the mornings,' Roz said in a high, tinkly voice. 'Don't bother him again. I'll help you with Meg.'

SIXTEEN

TO WHOM IT MAY CONCERN

Mrs Rosemary Welsh worked for me as my housekeeper for over four years. In that time she carried out her duties in my house — which included laundry and cleaning — with care and efficiency whilst being both an accomplished cook and a most charming hostess to my guests. She left me for personal reasons and it was, I am bound to say, with the utmost regret that I saw her go.

Professor H H Tunnicliffe M.A., Oxon.

PS I am currently taking sabbatical leave and am therefore unable to be contacted.

With this tissue of lies, written by herself, on writing paper from Professor Tunnicliffe's Oxford college, Roz secured a series of housekeeping posts, all of which were unsatisfactory.

From Daphne, she and Flora went straight to a wealthy woman in Warwickshire who had recently moved to country life in a Cotswold village and was now attempting to silence the crowing of the local cock through the courts. When the case came up, far from giving evidence on her employer's side against the cock, Roz switched to the other side and defended it. The cock held on to his situation but she lost hers.

Her next employer took exception to her mini-skirt. The one after that seduced her in it and his wife got rid of her. Some people were mean, others seemed mad. There was generally a catch somewhere if they were willing to take Flora.

She did everything for Flora. She 'borrowed' somebody's car. She sold somebody else's garden furniture. Being sacked had become a way of life. She left a trail of mayhem behind her.

Professor Tunnicliffe's house seemed to her now like a haven of peace and politeness. In a fit of guilt and remorse one Christmas, she posted him an heirloom teapot while she was in the middle of cleaning it.

'Always do what you feel is right,' Ma said. 'Once you've lost your good name, you've had it.'

What had happened to her? She'd never stolen anything while Ma was alive. Well, only once. She'd brought home Daphne's doll's eidy tucked into her own doll's pram.

'Oh, we seem to have Daphne's eidy! Ma rang up immediately and Roz returned it. Funny how that had been more shaming than the awful things she'd done since, because it never crossed Ma's mind that it was anything but a mistake. Being a housekeeper, had destroyed her. In trying to recapture her self-esteem, she'd sunk lower and lower and lower. She had nothing left to lose except Flora.

But most people liked Roz and that was their difficulty.

She was quiet and kind and eager to please. She was undemanding and biddable and happy to take a little less because they were taking Flora. In the nature of things they took advantage of her, as people do with servants. They couldn't believe it when she did them down.

One bewildered couple got in touch with Professor Tunnicliffe to discuss his experience with her. He told them he was very fond of Rosemary. He gave a weird little woof of laughter. He'd received a stolen teapot from her as a Christmas present. Had he by any chance received a pair of porcelain dogs, they enquired? No, he hadn't. Well, they'd better keep in touch in case he did.

And so Roz moved on to a Mrs Delphine Wright of Edgbaston.

Dee Wright, as she liked to be called, was a divorced woman in her forties who worked as Midlands sales representative for a refridgeration company. She travelled throughout the week, her job sometimes keeping her away for several days on end. Roz heaved a sigh of relief as they moved into her dreadful house, full of white laquered furniture and fluffy toy animals.

'I hate it,' said Flora, who was obliging her mother by trying out yet more paints at the kitchen table. 'And I hate her.'

'Yes, dog dirt if I'm not mistaken.'

'Ooh, you shouldn't say dog dirt!'

'I'm quoting, like Professor Tunnicliffe.'

'I heard you telling him off about it. You said it was better to invent things of your own to say than copycat from other people.'

'Yes, I did, didn't I,' Roz said, smiling to herself. 'How bold I was then.'

'Who said dog dirt?' Flora painted in a carrot for her three-legged horse.

'A philosopher.'

'What's a philosopher?'

'Somebody, I think . . . somebody perhaps who makes up new questions to ask.'

'Oh like me.'

'Yes. Be careful you don't make any marks on Mrs Wright's table.'

'Is my dad a philosopher?'

'No.'

Flora's beseeching face looked up at her again. 'He's never coming for us, is he?' Her lip twitched as she waited for the answer.

'Flor . . . I'm so very, very sorry but no, he's not coming.' She held the child with one arm and wiped her eyes on her other one.

'It's all right,' Flora said. 'I knew really.'

Roz took a deep breath. 'He's dead.'

'Yes.' As her tears plopped audibly onto the paper, she dragged her paintbrush backwards and forwards across the horse, until it was blotted out by black smudges.

Delphine Wright never cried or smiled. Her wide, tanned face was aggressively alert. The big, brown eyes missed nothing. Her laughs — bright, loud peals — came packaged with the neat little business suits, thrusting bust and thick dark burnished hair with which she wooed her customers.

'I want fun people in my house to keep it warm for me while I'm away,' she explained, always clackety clacking about on her stiletto heels as she talked, scarlet nails gleaming as she straightened a rug here or prodded a cushion there. 'I don't enjoy housework, Rosemary . . . I'm going to call you Rosie, that sounds more friendly, doesn't it? I don't enjoy cooking either but I make money at my job which buys me good clothes and smashing holidays and I don't see why I shouldn't pay somebody else to do my skivvying for me.'

'Very wise,' Roz said, actuely aware of her sensible shoes and charity shop skirt.

'I pour myself a whopping G & T when I come home. I like it with ice and lemon. I warn you I'm really murderous if there's no lemon! Then I take my shoes off, Rosie, put my trotters up and after that I get my second wind and feel fit to face the world again. D'you know what I mean?'

'I do.'

'My boyfriend and I entertain a lot together. He's married, unluckily for me, but we're working for the same company so no eyebrows are raised on that score. We only throw the occasional party here because I don't want my customers getting any funny ideas — give them an inch, Rosie, and they take five miles!' She laughed with bawdy appreciation. 'They're a rough, lecherous lot. There's no stopping them when they've had a few drinks. They'd have my granny if they got the chance.'

Roz and she might have been communicating through glass.

Some months later, when Dee Wright was away visiting abbatoirs in the Coventry area, the telephone rang a few minutes after midnight.

'Roz?' said a deep familiar male voice.

'Yes,' she answered warily.

'Darling Roz, it's Basil!'

'Who?'

'Basil. Basil Robson . . . your ex-partner,' he shouted in the old fulsome, fruity manner. 'Look darling, my call's running out. Can you take this number and ring me back?'

'No I can't.'

'Roz . . .'

'I don't want to talk to you.'

'Roz please, I've got something terribly important to say. Don't ring off. It's really jolly vital that you hear this.'

'Where are you?'

'I'm here, in Birmingham. I'm at the station . . . New Street. Quick! I'm going to get cut off and that's the end of my money. Here's my number.'

'Fucking, fucking hell!' she roared out as she rang him back.

He whipped up the phone at the other end. 'Thanks darling. You're a pal.'

'Basil, fuck off, I am not a pal and for God's sake don't keep calling me darling.' She began enunciating in a slow, deadly manner. 'I am still absolutely livid with you. I cannot believe how you did me down over our bureau. I don't want to be rung up at this time of night. It's not my house. If you've got something to say then just say it, but I don't know how the hell you got my number and I don't want any contact with you whatsoever until you start paying my money back. D'you understand that? I thought you'd gone to jail.'

'I came out yesterday. Listen, Roz, listen to me please. I've been thinking such a lot about you. I only need a bed for tonight. Can I just . . .'

'No.'

'I could hitch a . . .'

'*No.* Why should I?'

'Let me come for half an hour.'

'Basil, this is not my house, I keep telling you. You've ruined my life and Flora's. I hate you for what you've done and I don't want to see you. You'd better ring somebody else.'

'There is nobody else and I've got nowhere to go. I used what cash I had on the rail fare to get to you. I'll just have to kip in the street as I did last night if you won't have me.' He gave a weakly heroic laugh. 'Look here, let's talk about what I owe you because I've been left some money and I'm going to start paying you back. Give me your address and I'll be there as soon as I can hitch a lift. That's all I wanted to tell you. Put the kettle on, sweetie, I won't be long. I'm dying to see you again.'

'Bloody hell.' She started ranting to herself as she put the phone down and continued while she was making up the bed in the spare room. She couldn't believe she was going to get a penny from Basil Robson. He was going to raise her hopes and mess her about and she was going to let him because she couldn't leave him penniless out in the street. He was going to sponge off her and borrow more money. What a blithering ass she was!

By the time he rang the door bell, she had placed a carving knife under her pillow and looked up the number of the local police station to keep that beside her bed. She was beside herself with rage that he'd put her in this position. Why should she hobnob with the swine who'd wrecked her life? Who wanted to hobnob with a jailbird anyway? He'd be more self-pitying, more unstable. He might have gone mental. He could even be violent.

She did have an almighty shock when she opened the front door to find him standing on the step, smiling at her like a pale translucent copy of his old self. Prison had taken its toll. His ravaged face pleaded with her for acceptance.

'Roz!' His greeting had a kind of wounded heartiness about it as he took an eager stride forward to embrace her.

'Hallo Basil.' Avoiding his advance, she stepped back and stood aside to let him go in. She hoped her face was not outrageously disfigured with loathing.

Only one word came into her head as she took his coat. *Diminished.* He was diminished. He looked older, smaller, his hair was thin and grey, he was thin and grey and his suit was threadbare.

He would be surprised by her. She knew she must have changed. 'You look tired,' he said, with condescension and an equally irritating, mellow fruitiness of speech as if he'd left a four-car garage behind and an enviable wine cellar.

'It's nearly two o'clock in the morning and I'm in a very bad mood.'

'We'll soon get you out of that, sweetie.'

'I don't see how. You've put me in it.'

'Yes,' he nodded, following her as she led the way to the kitchen, 'I don't blame you.'

He was thinking, she thought, as she made him a pot of tea and two rounds of chicken sandwiches, that he'd better be meek lest his needs were not attended to. He kept glancing round the newly built-in kitchen, with all its gadgets, nodding at them and making a muffled 'Aha' sound down his nose as if clocking them up for future reference.

He still had manners despite incarceration with the lowest of the low. He kept on passing her the sandwich plate until he'd eaten all the sandwiches himself and she guessed he had had no food for hours. She knew he wanted a drink but didn't dare to ask for one, and she didn't offer any of Mrs Wright's whisky. She was determined not to indulge him by making sympathetic enquiries about his time in prison either. He'd asked for it and he'd got it. She didn't want to hear a single word about his problems.

While he was eating she'd been moving about, clearing up and doing little jobs. As soon as he'd finished she sat down at the table with him. 'Now Basil,' she said as pleasantly as she could. 'Have you a plan to pay me back?'

He put his hand out and gently shook her wrist. 'It is so nice to see you again, Roz. You don't look tired. You look wonderful. I'm surprised you're not married yet. I thought you'd settle down with that chap you were keen on.'

'Ivor? I've almost forgotten what he looked like. I don't think I'll marry. That's why I need the money. When can you pay me?'

'I'm going to start paying soon. In fact, I've been left quite a bit of money.'

'How marvellous for you . . . and for me,' she added quickly. 'Who is it? Is it a relation?'

'One of the old girls on the books of Seventh Heaven actually.'

'You mean she got married?'

'Yes.'

'Good Lord.'

'Yes.'

'Who was it?'

'Irene Crawshaw.'

'I suppose I do vaguely remember that name. Oh yes . . . of course! The one you got stuck with! Obviously a person of integrity.'

'Oh very much so . . . now you're teasing me. That naughty little smile of yours . . . how it brings everything back. You know you and I had a jolly good time together, didn't we.'

'Basil, please go on about Miss Crawshaw before I lose my temper.'

His eye gave a nervous twitch. 'She and I kept in touch. After that debacle, we didn't go back to the Cotswolds. I took her to The Mermaid at Rye.'

'D'you mean once or more often?'

'Well, I think we may have gone back there a few times yes. It's said to be haunted by the smugglers' ghosts but we never saw anything. She was terribly concerned when I got into that spot of trouble over my wives' alimony so, while I was in prison, I married her.'

'Good Lord,' Roz said again, wondering how many more surprises she could take without some of Dee Wright's scotch. 'This calls for a drink.' She went to fetch a bottle.

'Oh, I say, this is jolly good, darling,' Basil said. 'Can't we go and relax somewhere a bit more comfortable?'

'It's not my house, Basil.' She wasn't going to take him to her room.

'But there's nobody here. What's she like, by the way?'

'A business woman. Not unpleasant, though there's a distinct lack of radiance of the soul. It's actually ghastly taking orders from someone you don't respect, but I suppose you grow out of taking orders from anyone. Sometimes I can hardly breathe with boredom. Listen, if we don't go to bed in a minute, I'll never get up but just tell me quickly how it all happened.'

It was growing light by the time Basil stopped talking. It was ages since he'd had congenial company and he hadn't said all he'd got to say, by any means; but Roz shut him up. 'Come on. God help us! Look at the time,' she said, suddenly agitated. 'I'll never wake Flora for school. All I can say is I'm very, very sorry about Irene's death. I know how you'll miss her.'

There was a hint of the old caddish smile. 'Having the money makes up for a lot, you know. Funnily enough, it's a bit of a relief. It could have become extremely complicated. You see,' he confided, the drink causing a fatal slip, 'I was never legally divorced from my second wife.'

'Basil!'

'Yes, I know it's naughty but I took the view that I was already in the slammer so what the hell. If it came to light, the worst they could do was add a bit more time to my sentence. If I'd asked my ex-wife for a divorce, she'd have flown into another embittered frenzy and crucified me financially, so I risked it.

'But you're a bigamist.'

'Well, not any more, as it turns out, thank heaven.'

'It's something surely . . . false pretences?'

'No, it's all over now,' he said, with his new prison sniff.

Roz was already fast asleep when Basil entered her room and tried to get into bed with her. She woke up with a stifled scream.

'It's all right,' he said. 'It's only me. I've come to keep you warm.'

'I am warm.'

'Don't you want me to cuddle you?'

'No.'

He lifted the bedclothes. 'I'll just slip in beside you for a few minutes.'

'Basil, no you won't! Go back to bed.'

'Still frigid,' he declared disgustedly, tossing the covers back, 'I could change all that, you know. I could wake you up all right and you'd thank me for it. I'd make you plead for more.'

'Yes but we might wake Flora. Basil, chickey egg, I've been dwelling on the money . . . when will I have it?'

'Oh I don't know, I'll let you know, fairly soon,' he replied, rather dismissively, smoothing her sheet. 'I shall start making regular payments to you as soon as I can.' He let out an astonished oath as his hand was nicked on the carving knife. 'Good grief! What the hell's this?'

'A weapon for intruders. I always have it.'

'I can protect you from intruders. Why don't I just climb in in my underpants?'

'Please pipe down. I need ten thousand pounds right away. I want Flora to be able to go away to school, to do her O levels in peace.'

'Roz, dear heart, there's no way I . . .'

She cut across him. 'Ten thousand now, Basil, and the rest in monthly payments. We don't want my solicitor stirring up any more trouble for you by asking awkward questions. He as good as already knows you weren't divorced properly from your second wife.'

'Does he?' Basil sniffed. 'By golly I'm glad you warned me about that. We'd better say ten then, to start with, hadn't we. I've always felt guilty about it. Right.'

'Sleep well.'

'One more thing before I leave you . . . why don't we get married, Roz? Have you ever thought about that?'

'Thank you for asking, but I'm frigid.'

He blew her a kiss from the door. 'Can you lend me ten quid for tomorrow?'

'Yes I can.'

'And be a good girl, would you, there's an old chap called Alf who sleeps in St Andrew's churchyard at night. He was kind to me while I was trying to find you . . . that's where I slept last night. Can you give him a fiver from me when you're passing some time. I told him I'd call back to see him but I've got to get off to London in the morning.'

'I knew you'd catch me, I just knew it. Oh crumbs. All right. By the way, how did you find me?'

'I remembered your friend Daphne Phelps-Phillips. Her parents gave me her new number and her husband said he thought you were working for a Mrs D Wright in Birmingham. I rang at least ten people before I got you.'

'What did Daphne say?'

'She wasn't there and her husband didn't seem to know when she'd be coming back.'

SEVENTEEN

Alf, the churchyard dosser, came to tea with Roz on Thursday afternoons. He got off the bus at the corner and made his way slowly along Pinkerton Avenue to Mrs Wright's house but he was always dead on time. Sometimes Roz watched him from an upstairs window. He didn't walk. He shuffled. He put his right foot forward, drew the left up to it, right foot forward, drew the left up. She hadn't liked to ask what was wrong. His back was straight and his coat and suit were clean.

They sat in the kitchen and had cups of tea and cake and talked. Alf's subjects were films and bus routes, but their range expanded gradually to include politics, the activities of Flora and Delphine Wright and his difficulties as a man of no fixed address.

'You should have all sorts of benefits at your age,' Roz said.

'I'm not entitled.' He couldn't have help, he told her, because he didn't pay rates. He couldn't have social security because he didn't pay rent. She could see that someone like Alf was too gentle to go from counter to counter badgering and manipulating. He was too dignified. He would lose heart.

He was philosophical about being homeless. He'd worked in engineering factories since he was fourteen. One day he lost his job, lost his grip, and this was his retirement. The churchyard had been his home for two years. He kept a small cardboard box, filled with newspapers and sacking, concealed inside part of the church wall. He slept on a concrete slab.

After her promise to Basil to seek him out, it had actually taken her several weeks to locate Alf. He didn't come to the church until the pubs were closed and by that time the grounds surrounding it were dark and eerie. She had spied a shape lying huddled against the wall but she didn't dare go in on her own and disturb him. Eventually, she asked a neighbour, an American student who lived in digs nearby, to go with her. He was appalled when he saw the conditions in which the old man was sleeping.

'Surely that dosser would be better off in a doss house,' he'd declared, seizing the initiative in an energetic American way that would not have occurred to her.

'Yes, of course, I think he would,' she agreed, impressed. 'There is a hostel, Denby House, in Lariman Road, about half a mile from here. I could ring them up and ask if they've got any vacancies.'

'It's possible he may be a chronic alcoholic.'

'Well, we can't stand here whispering,' she'd said. 'Will you speak to him first? He might think I'm a prostitute or something and abuse me.'

'Sir!' shouted the student, leaning towards the lifeless bundle. 'Are you awake?'

Alf's head poked out timidly like a terrapin's coming out of its shell.

'What's wrong?'

'Sir!' the American repeated at full volume. 'It's a cold night. Would you like to go to a doss house?'

'Shall I be frank?' was the polite reply. 'No. Thank you.'

So Roz gave him a five pound note, and Basil's thanks, and they went home. Next day she took him an old blanket, half a bottle of wine and some rock cakes and left them tucked beside his cardboard box. But on the coldest nights, or when it was raining, she couldn't get him out of her mind. In the end she found out the name of the vicar of St Andrew's and rang him up.

'I do hope you won't think I'm interfering,' she said, 'but did you know that there's an elderly man sleeping in your churchyard?'

'Indeed we do know,' replied Father Nicholson. 'Yes, he's been coming here for ages. People leave a parcel of food out at Christmas and that sort of thing.'

'What I was wondering was whether there was anyone in the parish who would be able to give him a room?'

The vicar's voice changed. 'What?' he gasped impatiently, startled by the fatuity of her request. 'In this district? Oh no.'

'But people are always going on about compassion and campaigning?'

'No, not a chance, I'm afraid.'

'What do you think we can do?'

There was a small silence. 'What d'you mean . . . what do I think we can do? I don't quite understand you.'

'Well, I feel that he just can't be left out . . .'

'Oh look, Mrs Welsh, please take my advice . . . leave him alone. Leave him where he is. You'll never do any good with him. He's happy enough taking shelter in the church garden. He very likely has a drink problem. Many of them do. I expect that's probably his trouble.'

'All right then . . . thank you.'

'Thank you so much for phoning me. Goodbye to you.' And with a gush of relief that this absurd conversation was over, Father Nicholson rang off.

'I've got used to it now,' Alf said. 'As soon as it comes daylight, I get up. There's a café which opens at six o'clock and I go there for a cup of tea. Most mornings I wait for the bus and go for a ride round and sometimes in the afternoons I go to the cinema.'

Roz reacted to this as if such an existence was not out of the ordinary but, even if he could stand it, she couldn't stand it for him. 'Dee may know something we can do for him,' she said to Flora.

Flora giggled. 'He can have my room in the week.'

Flora was at home only at weekends now because she was a weekly boarder at her school. Her years of painting at kitchen tables paid off when she won an art scholarship which helped out with the fees. Roz felt relieved that she had more freedom to make a life of her own. It was frustrating for her always to be quiet and tidy in someone else's house now that she was growing up. When Basil started to pay off the rest of the money he owed, Roz planned to get a flat and a better paid job. In the meantime, she had to stay where she was for Flora's sake. As Delphine Wright did so much travelling, the job, though deadly, was bearable for a bit longer.

One Thursday afternoon Mrs Wright came home early as Alf was putting his coat on and about to go.

Roz heard her slamming the door of the Landrover and her heels clackety clacking on the gravel so she went to open the front door. 'Here comes Dee Wright now!' she called to Alf. 'I've been wanting you two to meet for ages.'

'Hi Rosie!' Mrs Wright said, bouncing in with her briefcase and yet more shopping bags filled with new clothes. She moved with as much zest as if she was starting the day, not finishing it but she stopped abruptly at the sight of Alf and raised her eyebrows. 'Is anything the matter?'

'Dee, this is Alf Hibberd . . . Delphine Wright. I'm so pleased you've come in time to catch him.'

Bandy, birdlike legs apart, neat and colourful as a toy soldier, Mrs Wright unsmilingly assessed the poor clothing and ill cut hair. 'Can I help you?'

Roz laughed at her formality. 'That's what I'm hoping. D'you know that Alf, in all this bad weather, is sleeping in a churchyard? I mind that, even if he doesn't. The point is, I wondered if you could think of anywhere for him to be?'

Her employer's red mouth took a downward turn. 'Denby House,' she said crisply. 'Anybody can get a bed there.'

'Not likely,' Alf answered genially, 'I've been in there. It's a dreadful place for thieving and the dormitories are full of drunks vomiting and urinating on the beds all the way through the night.'

Mrs Wright visibly shuddered and her mouth pulled into another disapproving shape as if the mere mention of such behaviour was as bad as the reality. 'Then I should go to the authorities, Mr Hibberd, if I were you.' She glanced about the hall as if checking that her possessions were untainted and still in place.

'No, no, it's no good, you see,' Roz explained to her. 'They ask if you've got Form PZ3 456 or something, and if you haven't, because you've got no fixed address, you've had it.'

'I'm sure Mr Hibberd knows better than we do how to deal with these problems.' Her red-nailed fingers drummed on the edge of the hall table.

Roz said nothing, not liking to point out that it was clear that that was precisely what he didn't know.

'Roz, I think I'll be off,' Alf said.

She went out to the gate with him to see him off, feeling as downtrodden and impotent as he must be feeling, and appalled that she'd caused him to be humiliated. 'See you next Thursday,' she said.

He drew himself up, looking most critical. 'I'll not come again, Roz. I'm surprised to see you with a woman of that type. I thought she'd be more like you.'

'Alf, of course you must come. I'm inviting you. You're my friend. See you then.' She gave him a little wave as she turned to go back into the house.

'I'm in here, madam.' Dee called out grimly. She was sitting on the sofa with her feet up and a large gin and tonic beside her. 'I've got something to say to you!'

Roz waited.

'I don't want that awful little man in my house.'

'But he's a friend.'

'I don't care what he is. I don't intend to come home to find the place stripped, thank you very much.'

'What are you talking about?' Roz demanded angrily. 'Alf wouldn't hurt a fly. I just want to help him a bit. Somebody's got to. He only needs a little push to get him back into normal life.'

'Well, my love, you can help him all you like but

you'll have to do it in the churchyard because he's not coming here.'

'My list of enemies is getting longer and longer,' Roz said bitterly to Daphne Phelps-Phillips, who was free for long gossipy chats again, now she was on her own.

'I can't say I'd welcome dossers in my house,' Daphne replied, 'I think you *should* be careful. I mean those people have not ended up sleeping outside for nothing, you know.'

'No, he's ended up outside because of his decent helplessness in the face of a rigid, ill-managed system. He doesn't know how to bend the rules and nobody's allowed the common sense to bend the rules for him so I'm going to. I want to make him a squatter so he can claim support with a fixed address and then I'm going to make an onslaught on the Council to get them to house him.'

'But where's he going to squat?' Daphne asked rather apprehensively.

'I've seen an empty house near here . . . well actually it's full of squatters but there's a ground floor room empty and they say Alf can have that. There's a little bed in it but no lighting or heating or anything. I'm going to take him there on Thursday.'

'You're not going to marry Alf, are you?'

'Don't be mad. He's seventy.'

'Look what I did.'

Neither Daphne nor Roz had ever referred to Glyn's behaviour with Flora, although Roz felt certain that it must have had something to do with the ending of their marriage.

'I left him,' Daphne told her, 'then I came back and

threw him out otherwise he'd have got the house. I learnt one useful thing with Glyn, anyway, and that is that you can't run a farm if you're fond of animals. He's gone back to work for Musker, I believe. I've decided I'm only having hens here. No cocks. He used to leave the cockerels out at night so the foxes would get them.'

'I'm glad he's gone.'

'I must say I never thought I'd be having a divorce. Aren't they frightening, these stages of life that one starts recognising? All the marriages take place, then babies are born — not in my case, thank God, with him — and the next stage is when the divorces start. Ivor's wife has left him, I heard. He doesn't seem to be getting much work.'

To the end of her days, Roz thought wearily, every time she heard Ivor's name she was going to go on jumping out of her skin. Even now, after all these years, if she put on her record of 'My Dearest Dear', she blotted out Mrs Mostance, Caroline Paul and Ivor's marriage and she was back in that unwelcoming sitting room at Ingledene, dumbstruck with love, listening to Ivor playing the piano and telling her,

> *... How slight the shadow that is holding us apart*
> *So take my hand*
> *I'll lead the way for you*
> *A little waiting and you'll reach my heart*

Had she been cursed at birth to relish only unrequited love? The dream seemed to be enough now. She was glad she had that at least, and that was all she wanted.

'Tim's taking Caroline out,' Daphne said. 'He's a surgeon now.'

'She always liked him,' Roz replied, feeling illogically betrayed by both of them.

'You people think you can have anything you want, don't you? That's why you don't get married. In many ways it's easier to be like me and have no choice. You just don't know what it's like to feel insecure.'

'Don't I?' Roz asked. 'You should try being virtually destitute, with a child and living in other people's houses as a servant. You become nothing because you are nothing. I'm like Alf.'

'In all conscience, Rosie,' Mrs Wright told her when she asked for more money, 'I can't raise you. I'm sorry. I mean, see it from my point of view. It's not everybody, is it, who would want a teenager in their house?'

'But you took us on.'

'Yes, I reckon many people would think I was a damn fool.'

'Flora's only here in the holidays now.'

'That's exactly what I'm saying to you, Rosie. You see, I really don't know why you're asking me for more money when she's not here so much.'

'Isn't it a bit mean to say that I'm not entitled to a rise when everybody else has them?'

'Mean . . . no. I don't think it is mean, Rosie, because I'm not a mean person. They get raises if they're worth it.' Mrs Wright's wide face seemed to expand visibly into the expression of a belligerent bullfrog. 'That's the law of supply and demand. You could earn more but you've chosen to opt out from the rat race, haven't you. I don't look down on you for that. We both accept we have a different outlook on life. I happen to feel I've got a lot of living to do, and I want to get out there and do it, and you want a quiet life. You don't do so badly out of it, do you? You get your quiet life and you have the run of my home while I'm away, but you've been abusing that privilege by bringing riff raff in here. Frankly, I'm not at all happy about it.'

At that point Roz knew she was perilously close to losing her job and stopped.

She started going for interviews then in Birmingham, but what she was offered was boring and ill-paid and what she wanted, she didn't get.

'Good manners will get you *anywhere*,' Ma said. 'How about going along looking very charming?'

It was a farce, sitting there in Delphine Wright's blouses and telling prospective employers she had run a marriage bureau a hundred years ago. She could hear herself, no longer that person, almost borrowing Mrs Wright's persona. The searching energetic stare, the bright peals of packaged laughter, yap, yap, yap, and she dropped in some of her expressions too like 'in all conscience' and 'ironclad guarantee' and 'dammit'. If they were wondering who she was, so was she. The thought of selling advertising space or demonstrating kitchen equipment made her bones ache with boredom. After each interview she walked off – with a plant or some toilet rolls – unsettled and depressed, only wanting to be wanted; and asking no more than that. There was no future in any of these jobs for her and therefore none for Flora. She hated herself and the whole world.

With Flora away, there was only Alf to need her. One morning, after a futile interview, she went into Rackhams to look for something useful for him in his new little squatter's room. He'd moved in reluctantly, almost to please her, she sensed, seeming to be apprehensive that it was somehow going to lead to him being placed in an old people's home. She hoped he'd lose his fear of the authorities now she was there to protect him.

She saw a blue towel. Out of habit she glanced about. She very nearly put it in her bag. But she couldn't do that to Alf. It had to be a present.

When she'd paid for it, and was drifting towards the doors to get a bus, she suddenly saw Dee. Already clutching some purchases, she was intently fingering a selection of silk scarves. With a dart of shock Roz rembered she was wearing her blouse! If Dee reached home first, which she undoubtedly would, in her Landrover, that embarrassing fact would be revealed. She could remember clothes she'd worn twenty years ago.

She was laughing to herself as she dodged out of sight and approached a make-up counter. 'Excuse me . . . I feel I ought to tell you . . . there's a short, dark-haired lady over there in a black coat and skirt . . . she's putting silk scarves into her bag. I've seen her doing this sort of thing before.'

'Thank you, madam,' the assistant whispered. 'I'll tell the store detective. She'll be stopped and searched when she tries to leave the store.'

EIGHTEEN

'Darling, if you pass your exams and if you do get into the art school, I want you to change your name when you go off to London.'

Flora laughed at her mother as she often did these days. 'What on earth are you talking about, mum?'

'I mean it. How do you feel about being called Cook?'

'*What*?' Flora screwed her face up, making slit eyes as Ivor used to do. 'D'you mean Cook by name and cook by nature or something? Is that what you're going to be called?'

'It's my mother's name, you know.'

'Oh . . . yeah. Well why? What have you done now?'

'I'm going to change your name by deed poll.'

'But I don't want it changed.'

'Listen, I want you to think about it. Please could you do this for me? What I want is for you to have a fresh start. I don't want you to be associated with me and all the messes I've made . . .'

'But you're my mother. I am associated with you. I love you.'

'If you love me, as I love you, then let me do it.'

'Well, if it matters so much to you, mum, why don't we

both do it? I'll do it if I go to London and you do it when Basil gives you the rest of your money back and you can afford to leave Dee.'

'It's a deal,' Roz said happily. 'I worry about all the dramas we've had and my bad reputation ... what if something happened to me and you were left with ... well, you see my mother had a very good name in the district. People will remember that.'

'Most people talk about their delinquent child,' Flora said, 'but I've got a delinquent mother. I know why you did everything you did. You did it for me, didn't you?'

NINETEEN

At last the Council gave Alf a room. But he didn't have long to enjoy it when he got it.

It was on the first floor of a battered old square of neglected, run-down houses, due to be demolished. Among all the boarded-up empty ones, there were a few houses left which showed signs of life. Of course, it had taken ages for Roz to get him even this place. She'd written again and again, cajoling and threatening the social services. She'd rung and badgered. She'd told them how asthmatic he was getting and how badly lame he was and that he could not possibly be condemned to return to the churchyard. Only when his ceiling caved in at the squat, and the owner was about to reclaim his house, had they offered him this alternative accommodation because of his age.

But it was furnished for him. He had light and warmth and a new confidence which came from coming in out of the cold. Far from feeling she was looking after him, Roz began to feel he was taking care of her. He loved Flora too and she went to see him whenever she was back from London.

'We've got a lot to thank your friend Basil the bigamist for,' Alf observed, more than once, as they sat together at lunchtime with pies and chips on their knees.

Roz laughed. 'You were rewarded, you see, for your good deed but I'm never going to tell him. I'm not giving an inch where he's concerned until I've got my money.'

That Alf's fantasy of somewhere to live had actually come true, had helped to revive her own belief that having enough faith could make things happen.

What seemed to her extremely ironic, in view of Alf's ecclesiastical links, was that the Church should finally come to him. Just before Easter he was asked if the Bishop of Edgbaston could borrow his balcony to speak at a Holy Week pageant, The Way Of The Cross. A procession, led by the bishop, would be marking the Stations of the Cross as it traversed the derelict square. Alf's balcony had been selected as the least likely to collapse. He remained his laconic self. He wrote in his diary for that day – 'Bis Ed'.

'I can't keep pace with your upward mobility,' Roz told him. 'Fancy a bishop coming here.'

'I don't believe in any of that,' he said.

But it was such a marvellous opportunity, Roz thought, to use this meeting between Alf and the bishop to stir up some publicity for other homeless people. She pondered on it then she rang the local paper and after that the bishop himself.

'Do you realise,' she said, 'that you're going to be preaching from the new home of an old man who has been sleeping out each night in a churchyard?'

'Oh really?' he replied. 'No, I hadn't realised that.'

'It must give you food for thought?'

'Indeed it does,' His lordship responded gamely. 'It immediately brings to my mind the story in St Luke's Gospel of the beggar called Lazarus, who lay at the gate of the rich man hoping to feed off the crumbs from his table.'

'Of course!' said Roz enthusiastically.

'And it came to pass, chapter sixteen, verse twenty-two, that the beggar died, and was carried by the angels into Abraham's bosom: the rich man also died,' the bishop went on fluently, 'and was buried.

'And in hell he lifted up his eyes, being in torment, and seeth Abraham afar off, and Lazarus in his bosom.

'And he cried and said Father Abraham, have mercy on me, and send Lazarus, that he may dip the tip of his finger in water and cool my tongue; for I am tormented in this flame.'

'Yes.'

'But,' said the Bishop, 'you will remember how Abraham said, "Son, remember that thou in thy lifetime receivedst the good things, and likewise Lazarus evil things: but now he is comforted, and thou art tormented."'

'Mm . . . I do remember it . . . not as you do, I'm afraid. I think you're saying how wrong it is for the gulf to be widening between rich and poor and this does seem to be a good moment to make some interesting and more personal publicity about it. The local paper is hoping for a few words from you on homelessness and Alf's part in the Easter pageant. They'll send a photographer to the house. But you're not saying that people like Alf must wait till they go to Heaven?'

'No, no, I'm not saying it. What I'm saying is that we must all do what we can. The individual gesture is what counts. We forget the homeless man in our society at our peril.'

'My leg is giving me gyp,' Alf complained, a day or two before the pageant. He was obviously in pain. His face was pale and strained and, although it was going to make her late for Dee, Roz went with him to the doctor in case he got into difficulties, or in case he didn't go.

The doctor examined him and wrote down 'irritation' on Alf's card. 'He thinks it's psychological,' Alf reported flatly, 'not physical.'

Mrs Wright was annoyed too. 'It's not good enough, coming back at this time, Rosie. You know I've got my boyfriend coming to dinner.'

With the advent of a new, more available boyfriend, Dee's routine had completely changed. She no longer disappeared to hotels for days on end, she was at home entertaining Josh and irritating Roz with a stream of high-handed notes pinned up round the house. 'Rosie, where the hell is my navy Jean Muir jacket? I need this cleaned by Thursday'. 'Please put the trash OUT before you go to bed otherwise it stinks the place out and I can't sleep in that atmosphere'.

Josh Garrett was several years younger than Dee. He had straggling dark hair, a lounging, insolent manner, loose leisure clothes, long legs and a lot of money. Every bit an ex-slaughterer, Roz decided. Dee, spending more than ever on her clothes, spared no expense in her efforts to impress him.

He arrived in his fast car, with the wireless playing at top volume through the open window. He sauntered in, joked suggestively with Dee and leered at Roz round the kitchen door as he tossed a parcel of meat onto the table. She could have prepared their supper in her sleep because it was always either prawn cocktail or vinaigretted avocado, (both made her retch), followed by steak. Josh imitated her voice when she took the food in and called her 'My Lady'.

Dee Wright sat there in clothes too young for her, trying to reclaim his attention and looking vulnerable. They watched television and went upstairs early while Roz washed up.

Even though she was entitled to a night off, Dee looked mildly put out, as if she was being done down in some way, as Roz set off to Alf's to await the Holy Week procession. Despite his leg pain, he'd been out for beer and coconut cakes for the Bishop. He'd laid the table with a checked cloth and found a lampshade for the naked light bulb.

Once or twice she thought she saw him wince with pain but he was straight-backed and he'd washed his old grey suit. The photographer arrived from the local paper and they sat down to watch at the one lighted balcony window.

At last they heard the procession coming! A deep murmuring of voices in the distance and the thud of three hundred pairs of striding feet belonging to priests, local people, students and children. And suddenly the flares they carried lit up the darkened square and the bishop splendid in his regalia.

They listened then for his step upon the stairs. Instead, to their astonished dismay, they heard his voice ring out below. He was addressing his audience from the back of a van.

'The homeless are increasing and there is a very real danger that sometimes we may even forget they exist. I wonder how many people in Birmingham tonight will have nowhere to sleep!'

'They're all bloody Trotskyites and layabouts in this square! Why don't you pack them off to Russia?' an angry heckler shouted across the Easter message.

And when his message ended, the bishop whirled about in his cloak and strode away, the crowds following. He'd forgotten Alf.

'Blimey, they've gone,' said the photographer.

'All that build-up for nothing!' Alf turned to Roz but she was gone.

She stepped out into the darkness on the landing and missed five stairs in her haste and at the bottom her legs gave way under her. She got up and ran, pushing past all the people to the front of the procession.

'Bishop, you've forgotten Alf! You said you were going to speak from his balcony. He's got cakes for you. He's the homeless man who used to sleep in the churchyard. The photographer is waiting for you too.'

The bishop stared at her blankly and seemed about to refuse then he suddenly made up his mind. 'Yes, I must have a quick word with Alf,' he said.

He went flying up the dingy staircase to the little room where the refreshments were waiting with his cloak swirling out and his retinue tumbling behind.

'How very kind of you,' he greeted Alf, 'I'm so sorry we can't stay long but we're in a great rush to stick to our schedule. My microphone packed up . . . that's why I didn't come up here.'

The photographer got a beaming picture of the two of them toasting each other although the bishop was only pretending and drank nothing.

'This is the first time I've met a bishop,' Alf said.

'But I gather you don't believe in God.'

'No,' he said, 'I don't want any prayers saying for me. I don't need 'em.'

*   *   *

Later that night his leg pain became unbearable. He struggled downstairs to ring Roz for help and collapsed in the street. A policeman found him and called an ambulance to take him to hospital. His left leg was amputated to save his life.

They called Roz at an early hour when she was still asleep. Dee Wright had switched the phone off in her bedroom and Roz flew downstairs in her nightdress to answer it.

She heard the news that Mr Hibberd had had an emergency operation. He'd given her name as next of kin.

'How is he?'

'I'm afraid he is rather poorly.'

'You mean I should come.'

'Yes, I think you should come.'

'As she put the telephone down, Josh grabbed her from behind. He'd apparently got up to answer it as well but she hadn't heard him on the stairs.

'Josh!'

At first she thought he must have drunkenly mistaken her for Dee in the early morning gloom but he was mauling her in a crude, insolent manner as if he'd expected her to have anticipated such an approach.

'Josh, stop it! What on earth are you doing?' She wrenched herself away from him and started up the stairs. 'I've got very bad news about that old man, Alf. Will you apologise to Dee and say it's an emergency. Tell her I've had to go to the hospital. I don't think they'd ask me to come if it weren't serious.'

Alf was lying with his eyes closed but after a time she suspected he was not asleep. He was shutting off the horror of what had happened to him. She talked a bit because she sensed he could hear her, but when his eyes did open they were full of fear.

'Come on, John! Time for your injection.' All the nurses made breezy squawkings round his bed in case he might respond.

'Actually, his name is Alf.'

'It says on his notes here that it's John. Alfred's his second name.'

'I know but he's always called Alf. Nobody has ever called him John.' It would be better still, she wanted to add, if you called him Mr Hibberd.

'Alf's got to take more nourishment than he's getting now. Can you help us to get him to start eating? He's not making the effort himself, you see.'

'If he does rally,' Roz asked the sister as they walked along the corridor together, 'how will he manage with one leg?'

'Oh, some people adapt very well. John could have many good years ahead of him. Of course, he won't be able to look after himself. He'll have to go into a home to receive proper care.'

'Why do you think there's no recovery at this stage?'

'We don't know yet. He had a clot in his leg. His stump is healing but John's not making the effort, you see. He doesn't want to get well.'

Every day she sat beside his bed, waiting for the moment he came out of his depression and decided he wanted to live. She bathed his face and told him bits of news about Flora. She held his hand imagining that sometimes the pressure changed.

'Don't leave me, Alf,' she said, but she knew he already had.

'I won't let you go to a home, you know. I'll look after you.'

She pondered on her empty words. What could she do for him now? She was as helpless in the face of the way things were as he was. She could only stand aside and let the worst happen, hoping he didn't live long enough to be taken away to a home. She'd got as used to being helpless as he had. Life had failed Alf. There must be one person in it who didn't fail him. He'd asked so little in that churchyard.

When she came again, the curtains were drawn round his bed and she hoped he was dying.

'They can't find out what's wrong yet,' a nurse said to her. 'He'll be having more tests tomorrow.'

His breathing was getting worse. 'Flora sends her love,' Roz said. 'She'll be coming to see you in a day or two. She's got into St Martin's School of Art. Isn't that marvellous?'

As she held his hand, a tear appeared in Alf's eye and lay glistening on his cheek.

He fell asleep soon after, rasping away with such difficulty. She stood up to pull the blanket over a pillow lying bunched up where his leg should have been. Instead, She suddenly held the pillow in her arms then pressed it over his face until the breathing stopped. 'Good luck!' she whispered and then she walked off.

She walked out of the hospital and all the way home.

Only Flora and she were at the crematorium to pray for him. ('I don't want any prayers saying for me. I don't need 'em.') There was a time when he needed much more than prayers but he had got used to managing with less.

TWENTY

Roz dreamt. But in these dreadful dreams it was not Alf who was murdered, it was Ivor's mother.

Roz recognised her because of the pony tail and the earrings dangling. When she passed the chocolate cake, her mouth was flat and stretched and her words came out as censoriously as they had on that day.

'I know what you did. I'll make sure everybody else knows too. I'm taking Flora from you because I'm her grandmother and you're unfit to be her mother. You're a murderer. You can never live that down. Never!'

And then Roz silenced her. Her death was not peaceful like Alf's.

When she woke, she reeled about at first in a fog of fatigue, trying to shake off the dream and establish reality. Was Alf dead? Was Mrs Mostance dead? Had the hospital discovered the cause of death? Were the police investigating? Where was Flora? Was she all right?

'Rosie, I think you and I need to have a very serious talk about what's happened.' Dee Wright came into the kitchen one morning, after Josh's departure, while she was washing up their breakfast things.

For one wild instant Roz wondered if Mrs Mostance had

been in touch. She put her hand out and held on to the edge of the table in case she keeled over.

'It's about Josh.'

'Josh?'

'Right.' Dee moved about in a sort of circle with her arms folded. When she looked at Roz again her expression was one of belligerent honesty.

'I'm going to put my cards on the table. I care a great deal about that man.'

'Yes. Do you?'

'Yes I do.'

'You're getting on well.'

'Rosie, Josh likes me because I'm his type and unfortunately he likes you because you're not.'

'Oh . . . God, Dee,' Roz shook her head.

'He wants a threesome.'

She screwed her face up in bewilderment.

'You're to be the hors d'oeuvre and I'll be the main course. Dee's thick hair bounced up and down as she laughed. Yap, yap, yap.

Roz wasn't laughing. 'Good Lord no. I wouldn't dream of it.'

'I need your help.'

'Dee, I can't help. I'm awfully sorry. As I said, I wouldn't dream of it.'

'I thought you might say that but Josh wanted me to ask you and I want to hold on to him. Humiliating, isn't it? What we come to.'

'Well . . .'

'Rosie, I think in that case you'll have to go. I can't have you in the house. If you're out of sight, I'm pretty sure you'll be out of Josh's mind. I'm not getting any younger and I've got to be a bit hard-headed where he's concerned. In short,' she said, trying to make it sound jokey, 'I want you out of here as soon as possible.'

TWENTY-ONE

'This is Mrs Elphick,' said Dorothy Bradman, matron and owner of Cliff House nursing home in Sussex, 'and her sister, Miss Preston.' She was introducing Roz to two well-dressed old ladies who were sitting in the comfortably furnished lounge with huge sunny windows overlooking the sea. 'Mrs Elphick was a sculptor and Miss Preston was a painter.'

'How lovely,' Roz said. 'How d'you do.'

'Hallo.' Mrs Elphick's face lit up into a sensationally sweet smile. She looked like some eager big-eyed little animal; like a chipmunk.

'I'm hoping Mrs Cook will be joining the board of Cliff House,' Mrs Bradman said. 'She'll be acting on the administrative side.'

Mrs Elphick smiled again. 'Everybody likes Cliff House.'

'Who's this?' demanded Miss Preston, who was dressed more dominantly in trousers and waistcoat. 'What are you people talking about. I can't understand you.'

Her sister put her arm round her. 'It's all right, dear. This is Mrs Cook. She's coming to look after us.'

'Is everything all right?'

'Yes it is.'

'It's all right?'

'Yes.'

'That's all right then.' Miss Preston laughed and they all laughed with her.

'Here comes Mr Cooper,' Dorothy Bradman said, as a frail figure carrying his panama hat and a newspaper entered the room.

Mr Cooper bowed to them. 'A word in your ear about our vegetables at lunchtime. I'm aware there's a general consensus these days that vegetables must be lightly cooked but they're a bit too raw for my taste. I experienced quite a lot of difficulty in chewing them.'

'We'll make sure you have a specially well-done selection, Mr Cooper,' Mrs Bradman assured him.

'This is our dining room over here,' she said to Roz, continuing their tour. 'Our residents take their food at regular times or in their rooms if they prefer it. We're usually full up, twenty-five at the moment. They're all pleasant in their different ways. Some of them can be a bit awkward at times if they're feeling below par.

'We only have one monster — there's always one — and that's Mrs Roper. She had a dreadful car crash at one time and she's crippled but I'm afraid hers is really a case of early senile dementia. I don't like to put her out because I don't know who else would take her. She's awfully naughty with us and the staff are terrified of her. No-one comes to see her, of course. She has one son but he very rarely comes here.'

'Are you going to like it, mum?' Flora asked.

'I love it,' Roz said. 'Elderly people are very moving. I seem to get on with them. It's funny, isn't it? If I hadn't met Alf, I'd never have realised what I was meant to be doing. I suppose it's one's luck in life whether that happens sooner rather than later. Getting my money back from Basil has made a great difference to me.'

'Can I come for a weekend in about a fortnight? I've just got some work to finish and I'm moving on Thursday.'

'Can I help? I can get up to London quite easily, you know.'

'No, no, I'm fine. People from college are helping.'

'Oh God, darling . . . I hear Mrs Roper's bell. She's a tyrant . . . none of the nurses will go because she's so rude to them. I'd better see what she wants.'

'You!' Mrs Roper said, when Roz opened her door. 'I've been ringing my bell for two hours but nobody ever comes.'

'I'm so sorry, Mrs Roper. How are you?'

'Are you a resident in this hotel or are you a member of the staff?'

'A member of the staff. I'm the deputy.'

'In that case, I'd like you to make up my bill. I shall be moving out this morning.'

'Oh . . . don't go,' Roz said. She went over to her wheel chair and sat down beside her. She couldn't help feeling sorry for this awful woman. She was alone, her mind was going, her face had been badly injured and she was too crippled to walk. No wonder her tongue was sharp. 'Is there anything I can do?'

'If you're Mrs Bradman's deputy, I must complain to you about the noise under my window. People gather there every day to talk about me. I can't tell what they're saying but they make a frightful disturbance and I want it stopped.'

'Oh, yes, I'm sorry. Some of the nurses eat their lunch on the patio. It's the only time they have to be outside. I'll ask them to be quieter.'

'I thought they were nurses. I could tell by their voices. I'm not having those common voices floating up to my windows.'

'D'you realise how upset the nurses get by the things you say to them?'

'They never come when I ring my bell, I know that.'

'They're too frightened.'

'They're too stupid. They don't do my dressings properly. My back is covered in sores.'

'We ought to move you a bit more. It's a lovely day. Why don't you let me wheel you into the garden?'

'That won't be possible. I'm waiting for my son.'

'Oh, I didn't know he was coming today.'

'He comes to see me every day.'

'I thought he was in London.'

'Of course he's in London. He's a star.'

As time went on Roz began to believe she really had made a fresh start. She enjoyed her job. One day she was going to work with people like Alf when she'd thought out how to do it. If only she'd listened to Tim, but of course she had to grow up first.

Now she was more grown up, she might telephone him. She knew he worked at Bart's. She could go up and see Flora's new flat and see him at the same time. The idea grew more appealing, the more she thought about it.

'My flat is great,' Flora told her. 'Eight people. It's on two floors and we all share the kitchen which is huge. My room is next to the landlord's studio. He teaches at Camberwell. He's even older than you.'

'In his dotage, I suppose. I hope he's responsible. Every time I ring you, I seem to get a black man who immediately says 'Sorry, dad, not in.' Are you out all the time?'

'Quite a lot. That guy calls everyone dad. He's a dancer when he gets work but there's one old bum,' Flora suddenly whispered, 'who keeps stealing the last egg out of my food cupboard. He's a painter too. He really stinks. He can open any lock with a piece of silver paper.'

'Flora, please be careful. I don't like the sound of him at all.' The worry was much worse, Roz thought, if you'd led a rackety life yourself. 'Are these men all right?'

'Oh, they all try it on, don't they, and then you can become good friends. Oh yes, I was going to tell you, there's another one who works in the box office at Sadler's Wells. He gives me tickets sometimes so we can go when you come. I think you'd really like him. He used to be a singer and he keeps inviting me into his room to listen to naff old records. He's writing his own lyrics now and trying to crack the pop scene but he's probably too old-fashioned. Anyway, I'll introduce you. He's a bit of a drinker but he's very handsome.'

'D'you mean introduce me with a view to friendship and marriage?'

Flora laughed. 'Yes.'

'Well, couldn't we hold on for one with better prospects? But my darling, I suspect I'm past all that stuff. I couldn't stand it again.'

When she rang Tim, she'd find out, whether she could or not. She was longing to hear his reaction to her changed circumstance.

'Roz? I don't believe it!' he said, when she eventually got him.

'How are the lobotomies?'

'Well, they're letting me loose at last. D'you want one? Is that why you've rung me?'

Her past seemed to loom up again and envelop her. 'No, I was just wondering . . . Flora's in London now and I'm a director of a nursing home in Sussex. Shall we meet when I come up to see her?'

'Sure. That would be good. I'd love to see you both. You know I'm with Caroline now? We could all meet for a drink. We're getting married soon.'

'Tim's going to marry Caroline Paul,' Roz said to Flora.

'Oh, what a pity,' she replied. 'I thought you and he were dead right together. He really loved you, didn't he.'

'I don't know.'

'You know the one in the box office I told you about?'

'What?'

'You know . . . the older man who writes these lyrics about his lost love who had a baby with someone else . . .'

'Oh yes, my intended?'

'Yes.'

'It's no good to me,' Roz said, laughing, 'if he loves another.'

'Oh, that was all years ago. I expect he's just using the experience for his lyrics. You'd really like him. I know you would because he's . . . he's *vulnerable*.'

'A lame duck? I don't want it.'

'You do,' Flora insisted. 'You *do*. That's what you do want. It's only the defenceless who turn you on. If anyone is up and strutting, you go for the jugular.'

'Nonsense.'

'Well, look what happened to Tim. Look what happened to the people we worked for.'

'But I was at my lowest ebb . . .'

'Yes, but I think he is, you know. I cook lunch for him on Sundays now. He calls me "ducky" and spouts all this stuff about all the years that we're apart, I pray that love lives in your heart. He tells me to write it down and I just laugh at him. It's quite touching, isn't it. He says he's a womaniser.'

'Oh Flora, be careful. Don't get yourself tied up with an old lag.'

'Old lag! He's terribly attractive,' Flora said. They got into an argument about it so the subject wasn't mentioned again for some time. She hoped Flora wasn't going to fall for this bum . . . old, spongeing, drinking and womanising. What a shock. She could only hope to prevent it by saying nothing.

When Flora did bring him up again, she felt most relieved.

'That box office man, well, actually, he's the most marvellous singer, I've discovered . . . but what I was going to tell you is that his mother lives in your nursing home.'

'What's her name?'

'Mrs Roper — that rude one! We're coming down to see you.'

Roz had wheeled Mrs Roper down the garden so that she could look out over the water. She wasn't looking. She was dozing, her sun hat tipped over her eyes.

If her son actually was coming today, Dorothy Bradman said with some scepticism, it would be the first time for about nine months. While she waited for Flora, Roz was hacking at the rough grass which had grown over the edges of the narrow cemented path to the cliff.

She was so deep in thought, she didn't hear Flora and her father coming towards them. Ivor reached his mother first.

'Hullo mother,' he said and kissed her. 'How are you?'

'Do I know you?' she said.

'There's my mum,' Flora told him, pointing to her mother, who was kneeling in the grass with her back to them.

Ivor released the brake on his mother's wheel chair ready to push it.

'Would you please leave me alone! I'm waiting for my son.'

'Mum!' Flora called. 'Here we are! Here's Ivor.'

Very slowly Roz stood up and turned round.

As she and Ivor stared at each other, his mother gave her wheelchair an angry shake. 'I'm sorry. I can't sit here all day. Take me to my room.' She bounced on the seat and set the chair moving.

Too late, they ran to stop her. She bowled down the little cement path, tipped over the cliff edge and disappeared.